The Road to the River

Helen Armstrong lives with her husband, two dogs and a cat in Wiltshire. She spends her free time hill-walking, bird-watching and learning to play the harp. *The Road to the River* is her second book for children, following the successful *The Road to Somewhere*.

The Road to the River

Helen Armstrong

Illustrated by Steve Dell

Orion
Children's Books

First published in Great Britain in 2002
by Orion Children's Books
a division of the Orion Publishing Group Ltd
Orion House
5 Upper St Martin's Lane
London WC2H 9EA

Typeset at The Spartan Press Ltd,
Lymington, Hants

Printed in Great Britain by
Butler & Tanner Ltd,
Frome and London

ISBN 1 84255 031 4

To Annie,
who read every word twice over

CHAPTER 1

I love adventure. Ratties do.

I am a ratty, round, and brown, and sharp as my two front teeth. Which is very sharp. I sit here, high on the roof of the cowhouse in the early morning sun. I am waiting for something to happen. The cowhouse is in the City Farm – that is where I live now. It is a good place to be. But I love adventure and there is not much of that.

I can see my friend Cow down there on the little patch of green. Cow is my oldest friend in all the world and she is famous. As soon as the gates are open, people will come and stroke her nose and take her photograph. Over there is Woolly Woolly Baa Lamb. He looks so curly and round but he is a fierce lambkin. People come to photograph him too.

They don't take photos of me. No they don't. And a good thing too. Ratties are a secret folk. That way we live a long time and have more fun. Except now. Now I am bored.

It is early morning. Hat Man has arrived. He is the person in charge. He wears a big hat on his head whether it is raining or snowing or shining bright.

Hat Man has gone to let out the chickens. He has a bucket of chicken food in one hand. He opens the wooden door of the henhouse.

'Screeech!' shout all the chickens together.

'Aaaah!' shouts Hat Man.

Out rush the chickens. Out they pour. Like a white feather flood. They fly, they leap. They scrabble over Hat Man with their clawed chicken feet. They flap their wide chicken wings.

Hat Man drops his bucket. He puts his arms over his face. In two blinks he is on his back in the mud and all the chickens are sitting up a tree.

I jump up so quick that I almost fall off the roof. Cow stares from her paddock. Woolly Woolly Baa Lamb dances on his hard hooves behind his fence. 'What is happening?' he bleats loud and fierce.

'Where am I?' asks Hat Man.

One of the other helpers on the farm comes running up. 'You are knocked over by hens,' says she.

'By hens!' says Hat Man. 'What is the world coming to?'

Hat Man gets up. He turns round and wipes the mud from his clothes. He stares at the chickens and he waits.

They stare back. Chickens do not look very bright ever, any day. But today, their eyes are popping from their heads. They do not look as if they know which way is up.

'What has happened?' asks Hat Man. 'Chicken friends, you do not seem yourselves this morning.'

'Ourselves!' squawks Chief Hen.

'Ourselves!' squawk all the others behind her.

'We are lucky to be alive and clucking,' says Chief Hen.

'So lucky!' say her friends in a chorus.

Hat Man is puzzled. 'What do you mean?' says he.

'The Bad Things came,' the chickens mutter through their pointed beaks. 'They came last night into our henhouse. They have white teeth, and bright eyes. They sang. They danced.'

Well, all this is babbling. That is what I think. But Hat Man is a kind man and wants to know.

'Tell me,' he says.

'The Bad Things – that is what they said they were!' The hens cluck the words out in a sort of rush. 'They flashed their teeth at us. They danced in circles. We flew onto our top top perch. We hung on tight. We shut our eyes!' Their hen voices are getting higher and higher.

'The Bad Things said they would get us!' says Chief Hen. 'Soon, they said. No pet is safe they said. We will all be chopped up by white teeth. That is what they said!'

Chief Hen stretches her neck. She tries to settle on her branch. But she cannot do it. She trembles too much. 'They frightened us,' says she. 'We are not safe.'

She falls silent. The other hens all sit behind her in the tree like a white cloud and say nothing at all.

Hat Man shakes his head. 'This is something new,' says he. 'But you will be safe tonight I promise. I will put you in the spare room in my house. I would like to see someone hurt you there!'

The chickens open their eyes a bit wider. Their feathers fall smoother on their backs. They begin to breathe easy. Hat Man will keep them safe.

But where does that leave the rest of us? Perhaps Hat Man was not listening as sharp as me. No pet is safe – that is what Chief Hen said. No furry pets nor feathered hens neither. None safe. So what about Cow? What about Woolly? What about all my friends?

The Farm looks safe as can be. But it is not. That is clear.

I see Cow standing quiet in her patch of green. Cow is a thinking kind of cow. And thinking is what she is doing now. I can tell.

Woolly is standing by her. He is frowning and waving his curly tail. 'Come on down Ratty!' he bleats. 'We need to talk.'

I turn to scramble down off my roof.

I have not got to the roof edge when I hear a voice.

Very close by.

'Ratty? Are you Ratty?' asks the voice. It is a sharp, scrapy kind of voice.

'Me?' I say. 'Who's there? Who's there?'

I look about me. I have heard no feet, no flutter, no movement. Who is speaking?

Then I see him. It is a Beetle. He is big and glossy black. He has two prongs on his head. He is in the gutter of the cowhouse roof. He cannot get out. But he is trying and trying. That is Beetles all over.

I remember Woolly. 'Wait a minute Woolly,' I call down to the paddock, 'I have a visitor!'

'Visitor!' snorts Woolly. 'A likely story!' And he whisks his tail and stamps one hard hoof.

Then I scamper over to Beetle. I peer at him as he struggles below me in the gutter.

He is cross. His back legs are pushing and pushing but he cannot get up. He stops a moment.

'Are you Ratty?' he gasps. One more push. 'Well are you?' he screeches.

Then he gives a last push. Up he pops and stands on the roof. He is breathing a bit heavy I must say.

'I am Ratty,' says I.

'You could have said so sooner,' says Beetle. 'I've come far enough. Could do with a few manners when I get here!'

'I am sorry,' says I. 'Today has not started well. Something is going on and I don't know what. Something nasty!'

'Nasty?' says Beetle. 'Nasty? Of course something nasty is going on. Why do you think I've come to find you? Nastiness and badness, that's what.' He looks about him in a worried sort of way. 'Here already?' he mutters so soft I hardly hear him. 'Everywhere soon, everywhere.'

'I am pleased to meet you of course,' says I, trying to be polite. 'But why are you looking for me?'

He turns his pronged head towards me. His eyes are sad. 'I come from Minka,' he says. 'She is in trouble.'

'Minka!' I almost topple backwards.

Minka. Our mink friend, our river friend. If you have heard the story of our great adventure you will know Minka. She helped us. She led us from the cold river side to the edge of the city. I have never seen her since – not for months and long months.

'Minka in trouble?' My voice trembles. 'How? Friend Beetle, tell me how?'

'She is kidnapped. She is trapped,' says Beetle. 'By the Bad Things.'

6

My heart skips a beat at this. That is the second time this morning I have heard of the Bad Things.

'Bad Things,' I say. 'Who are the Bad Things? I have not heard of them until today.'

'I do not know who they are,' says he. 'But Minka sent a message to you.'

He closes his Beetle eyes and opens his Beetle mouth. He breathes deep. Then a strange noise comes from his dark and shiny mouth. 'Help me! Help me!' It is high and piercing and full of fear.

It is Minka's voice. I remember it well. Minka's voice from Beetle's throat.

Then Beetle shakes himself. He opens his eyes and says as plain as plain, 'That is her message. Part One.'

'Oh Beetle,' says I. My fur stands on end. My skin shivers as if with cold. 'Oh Beetle, that is bad indeed.'

'Part Two is this,' says he. He closes his eyes again. Once more his shiny mouth opens in a high and trembling cry. 'Watch for Number 29! Fear him!'

Then Beetle closes his mouth. He shakes himself again. He is only Beetle and nothing to fear at all.

'Where is Minka?' I ask. 'Where did you see her? How can I find her?'

'I was scratching around an old and dusty place,' says Beetle. 'Far away. Over the river. She saw me and she said – I need someone who can fly and scramble. I need someone who can go where big things cannot go. That is me, you know,' says Beetle. 'Find Ratty, he will help me,' says she. She told me where you were and I have found you! It has taken six light days and six dark nights.' He smiles a proud and beetly smile.

'A long time,' says I. I think of Minka. Six days is a long time to be trapped. Too long. 'How is she trapped?' I ask.

'She is in ice,' says he. 'Ice – I think. Thick and clear and hard.'

'Ice!' He cannot be right. Not ice. It is the bright summertime. But he has seen her, not I.

'How can I find her?' I ask.

'She says – look for her by the brown stream on the great river side. That is what she says. Of course I do not go near rivers. I am not a water beetle, oh no. Water beetles!' he snorts. 'Nasty slidy swimmy things they are! No, I am a nice dry land beetle. I know nothing about streams, brown or pink or green or whatever,' says Beetle.

'I know the river,' says I. 'I know it. Though I am not sure how to find it from here.'

I think of Minka. Minka with her pointed face and glossy pebble eyes. Trapped in some strange and hidden place. I chew my whiskers. The hens were right. No creature is safe now. But who is Number 29?

Then I remember my manners. 'Dear Beetle,' I say, 'you have come a long journey. You must be hungry.'

'I have. I am,' says Beetle.

'You have done a great thing,' I say to him, 'I am proud to know you. My friends will want to meet you. I shall carry you to them and find you food.'

I help Beetle onto my back. I slide down the drain-pipe. I step past the white chicken cloud in the tree. I scamper into the green paddock. I look around for Cow and Woolly Woolly Baa Lamb. Where have they gone?

I find Cow – but what a surprise! She is in one corner of the paddock. She has her four feet in four separate buckets. A person friend is washing her with soapy water and a big sponge. Then I remember. Cow is going to a Show. She must look her best. Woolly is watching. He is waiting his turn to be washed.

Cow is giggling and smiling. Just at this minute she has forgotten all about the Bad Things and the hens. That is clear.

'Cow,' I call out, 'and Woolly too. Meet brave Beetle here. He has brought us news of Minka.'

Cow whisks her clean clean tail. She steps carefully out of her buckets.

The person with the sponge leans back. 'Want a break now?' says she. 'I'll come back in a few minutes,' and off she goes.

Cow trots up. 'News of Minka!' says Cow. 'Can we see her? Where is she?'

Up comes Woolly. He dances on his hard little hooves and whisks his tail.

'Minka is a good friend,' says Woolly. 'I hope she is well.'

Then they see my face. They look at me and then at Beetle.

'Listen,' says I, 'soon you will know as much as I do.'

I tell them all that Beetle has told me. When I have finished I shake my head. 'Beetle says Minka is trapped in ice! That is odd,' says I. 'And then Minka says beware of Number 29. Beware of him. I do not know what that means either.'

Woolly goes very still. He is like a sheep of stone. 'Number 29,' he says very quiet. 'A creature with a number. Numbers is bad news, Ratty. We know that.' He shakes his curly head. 'How did he get his number? It is bad news for him. And bad news for us maybe. That is what I think.'

I look at him and remember. He is right about numbers. Woolly and Cow both had numbers once. Sometimes I think I still see Cow's number like a shadow in her fur. Woolly's number fell out as his whole woolly coat fell off, piece by piece, in the springtime. They are glad to be rid of them. Numbers is no good news at all, that is what they say.

Cow is thinking of other things. 'We must find her, that is the main thing,' says Cow. 'Yes, we must. But Ratty, how can a big cow like me do that?' Her eyes fill with tears. 'People will stare and point if I step outside the farm gate. Hat Man will notice straight away.'

Woolly is standing next to her. His face is glum too. 'Ratty,' says he, 'I am like Cow. People notice me.' He sinks his woolly head almost to his knees. 'There is only one answer,' says he. 'You must go to find her, Ratty. And you must go without us.'

Cow and Woolly are brave as lions. But they cannot go to find Minka. They are right. There will be lots of hiding and creeping if we are to find Minka. And they are not hiding creeping things. I am the one who must go.

I feel a shiver down my back. 'You are right,' I whisper. 'I must go. We ratties are good at hiding. No one sees us. I am not so small as Beetle but I will find Minka if anyone can.'

Then Cow lifts her head. She has thought of something. Her eyes shine once more.

'Remember!' says she. 'Woolly and I are at the City Show tomorrow! We are going in the trailer tonight. Get to the Show, Ratty, and we can help you! Come and find us there. We will be waiting.' She smiles her soft broad smile. 'We are your friends, Ratty. Find us and all will be well.'

'Oh yes!' cries Woolly. His eyes gleam blue like winter sky. 'Bring us news tomorrow. Find us at the Show. Then we can all help Minka!'

'I will find you if ever I can,' says I. 'I will.'

Cow stares around at the Farm and the animals and Hat Man working by the gate. She shakes her head sadly. 'This is such a good place,' says she. 'People are so kind to us. There is no badness here. Not till this morning. Where has the badness come from?'

'I do not know,' says I. 'But we must find out. And we must stop it!'

Cow nods her gentle head. Then looks around again. Her head is the highest and she sees the most. 'There are no visitors here yet,' says she. 'Now is the best time for you to go.'

'I will be off at once,' says I. 'Beetle has told me where to look for Minka. I shall go now. Goodbye, dear friends. Look out for me tomorrow at the Show.'

'Goodbye,' says Cow. 'Good luck. How I wish I could come too.'

'Goodbye,' says Woolly. He shakes his head sadly.

Beetle is munching scattered grains of chicken feed. He waves his antlered head at me. Then he goes back to eating.

I scurry off. My heart is beating hard in my ratty

chest. I have no plan. I do not know which way the river is.

But I can find it I am sure. I will find Minka. And I shall watch for Number 29.

CHAPTER 2

It is clear morning now. I had better move quick and soon. Visitors do not like ratties. I run towards the farm gate. Hat Man is putting up a poster on the gatepost. I scamper past him. Then I stop and turn back and look.

I look and look again. Since we came to the City Farm I have learned the words on the stable doors and the gates and on the food bins too. But I cannot read this notice. There are too many new words in it.

'Should I read it for you?' says Hat Man. I nod and this is what he says.

'Furry Pets and Farm Friends
Your City Show
Come one, Come all to Greeber's Ground
A Family Day Out!'

'It should be good,' says Hat Man. 'Your friends will be there, you know.'

'I know,' says I.

Hat Man looks at me in a funny way.

'You look worried, Ratty,' says he. 'And you look as if you were in a hurry. Are you off somewhere?'

'Mmmm,' is all I say.

Of course I am off somewhere. But I do not know where to start.

Hat Man laughs. 'If you want a trip out,' says Hat Man, 'take a bus. That's the way to see the world!'

He laughs and laughs at this. He thinks he has made a good joke. But why not? That is what I say. Ratty legs are very short. We cannot run far. A bus! What a good idea.

I know what buses are. They roar past the Farm day after day. Some of them are red, some are yellow. Some are very high, like houses almost. Some are long and square-shaped. I have never been on a bus but I can start now. Why not?

So I nod my head to Hat Man. Then out I go into the street.

Hat Man goes away to his other jobs. I tuck in behind a waste bin and watch the bus stop. It is so strange being on my own. I wish that Cow or Woolly was here with me. But they could not hide here. That is the truth. This bin is only big enough for a ratty. A little ratty. It is not quite big enough for a fat ratty like me. I have to squeeze in tight to stay hidden.

I see one bus arrive. It has a big number on its front. Number 77. It slows down but no one is waiting so it goes right past. That is no good. Even a ratty needs a bus to stop and open its metal door.

After a while another bus pulls round the corner. This one stops. Lots of people climb out. There are feet and boots and bags and talk. I tremble behind my bin. I cannot run across the pavement through that crowd. Someone will see me.

The doors clang shut. The bus roars and off it goes.

I am worried now. How can I get onto a bus? It may not be so easy.

Then a lady appears down the street. She walks up to the bus stop. She has two big bags and a long skirt. It couldn't be better. I can hide behind her! Then I can skip aboard easy beasy.

Round the corner comes a high yellow bus. On its front there are big white letters. Number 29.

This is the bus I want. That is clear enough. The very number. Watch out for Number 29 says Minka. I have, and here it is.

My heart beats in my furry chest. Perhaps the bus will take me to danger. But I will not turn back now.

I must get on this bus somehow, anyhow.

My luck is in. As the bus comes closer, the lady waves. She wants this bus. So do I.

Crunch, bang, the bus stops.

'Come on board, lady!' shouts the driver. He sits just inside the door up two big steps. He does not see me. 'Come on board and good morning to you!'

'Morning!' shouts the lady. She picks up her bags and puts them on the top step. Then up she goes after them. She pays the driver. Flash. Patter. Up I go, like a brown streak of lightning. Up and in.

I run along that bus so fast that even a bright-eyed person would blink and miss me. But there are no bright-eyed people here. There are only three people on the bus and they are dozing.

Under a seat I go. I crunch up small and tight against the bus side. I wait. The roar starts up, the bus shakes like Farmer's tractor. Off we go.

It is so loud down here on the floor. So rattly too and shaky. The air whistles past me from the cracks in the door. I cower down and wait under my seat.

The door opens at the next stop. There is a clump, clump on the bus stair. I see another lady step in. She takes a seat opposite me. She has a bag too. A big heavy bag upon her knee.

I look again.

There is a head sticking out of the bag. It is a round

head and yellow and bald. It has pointy ears and bulging eyes.

The eyes look straight at me.

'I see you,' says Round-head. Her voice is high and squeaky. 'I see you I do. A ratty thing under a seat. There you are! There you are!'

'Shush, shush,' says the lady with the bag. 'Be quiet, my little pet. Stop this yapping.'

Round-head has a high squeaky bark. She is a doggo. I cannot believe it. A tiny doggo. Hardly a doggo at all so wee she is. So wee, so bald, so squeaky. But she is a barking doggo and that's for sure. I know what to do now.

'Under the fur,
Friends are we,'

I hiss as loud as I dare. 'Friends under the fur, little doggo. That's what.'

You will remember this rhyme. Wall-Eyed Doggo taught it to me and my friends at the start of our first adventure. He was a two-faced doggo but the rhyme is a good rhyme for all that. It works now.

Round-head freezes. She stares. Her round eyes go so big I think they will pop out of her face. Her tiny ears shake with excitement.

'Oh ratty,' squeaks she. 'A ratty who knows doggo rhymes. A wild ratty. A friend under the fur. Oh joy!'

Round-head has pushed her head further out of the

bag. She is not quite bald I see. Her fur is very very short and yellow and spotted with grey.

'You are on the run!' she squeaks. Then she starts to sing in her creaky squeaky voice.

> *'Running far!*
> *Running free!*
> *Lucky you!*
> *Lucky me!'*

What is Round-head thinking of? I do not need a singing doggo. That is for sure.

'Not lucky. Not free at this minute,' I hiss. 'Stuck! That's what I am!'

It is true. We have stopped at two more bus stops now. At each stop, more people get onto the bus. I am still under my seat. All round me there are shoes and boots and legs. My ratty heart is racing. I must get out and soon.

Round-head stares. People push along the passage of the bus. She moves her yellow tiny head this way and that to keep her eyes on me.

'You are a fidget today,' says her person. 'Keep still, my darling.'

Round-head sees the look in my eye.

'You are going soon!' says she. 'I see it. I see it. I shall come too!'

'No! No! No!' I squeal. Almost too loud. The feet in the passageway move a bit as if they wonder where

the noise comes from. 'No! You cannot come. Stay there. Stay. You are a pet. This is wild work.'

'Wild work!' sighs Round-head. 'That's for me.' She half lifts herself out of the bag.

I hear the engine noise change. I feel the bus slow down. It crunches to a stop. The doors clang open.

Out I leap!

Out of my shelter! Out from the seat! Off I go!

Into the passageway of the bus.

Over those feet. Scamper scamper scamper.

Claws scratching on shiny shoes. Claws pushing on ankles. Leap after leap after leap. To the open door.

'Aaaaaaaah!'

The noise follows me.

'Aaaaaaaaaaa!'

Each person starts to yell. Each person starts to scream.

'A rat on my foot!'

'A rat!'

'A raaaat!' They all scream together loud and long.

My ratty ears hum with the noise but I am almost to the door.

'I'm coming too!' squeals Round-head. 'Eeeeeeh!'

Out of her bag she leaps on her tiny curved legs. Out and down in two jumps.

'Here I come!' squeals Round-head.

'Oh brave darling!' screams her lady, up on her feet now. 'She is chasing that horrid rat! Darling, come back! Brave pet, leave that nasty rat alone!'

Round-head is stopping for no one. She is out. She is free. She is not going back. I am on the hard road now. She is just behind me.

'Where now?' she squeaks.

I pause for just one ratty breath.

I look one way. I look the other. There are people everywhere. There is noise and cars and smell and the hard clack of shoes on paved ground.

Where now indeed?

Right ahead of us I see a big door. It is as big as Farmer's barn door. It is open wide. There is light inside, and bright bright colours.

'Here!' I shout. 'This way!'

I hear Round-head's paws pattering behind me. I hear a voice. 'What is that? There! It can't be ... !' Someone has seen us.

Faster still I run. We are inside the big door now. Across the floor I see metal stairs, shining metal steps, straight ahead.

I leap up onto the first step. It is hard and cold and shiny. And it floats upwards like a cloud. The stairs are moving!

I stare back at Round-head Doggo. She has just jumped onto the first step. Behind her another new step appears. She is moving up after me. We are carried upwards, swift as birds.

Round-head's eyes go as round as her apple head. She flashes her white teeth. 'I like this!' says she.

I am already at the top. The metal step goes flat and slides under some spikes. I leap high and quick over them. I look about me. It is quiet and light and bright. There is a thick softness on the floor.

Round-head is close behind me. She rises over the stair-top and leaps to my side.

'This way,' I squeal.

Someone may see us. But speed may save us. Quick as a flash I go. Zip this away, zip that. Round-head runs after me.

'In here,' says I. I dive into the first shelter I see.

Now I have time to look around me. To sniff and smell. And listen too.

We are under a kind of hanging rack. A sort of haystack, made of coats. Yes, coats. They hang all round us from thick bars above our heads.

They do not smell of people. They are not like Farmer's clothes or Hat Man's clothes. These clothes are new as new. They smell of newness. They smell of long roads, of lorries, of boxes, and cleanness. They have bits of paper hanging from them.

All around the room hang other clothes, jackets, dresses, trousers. Some hang in islands in the middle of the room. That is where we are now. Under one of the islands of clothes in the middle of the room.

I peer out. Across the wide bright space. My ratty heart sinks to my ratty paws. I am stuck here. I am lost. I am far from the river. I am far from Minka. What can I do now?

CHAPTER 3

I am stuck in this strange place. How can I save Minka now?

I sit in a sad ratty lump under the coats. Then I turn my head and stare glumly at Round-head.

'We have got time now and lots of it,' says I crossly. 'So could you tell me who you are, my round-head friend? I have never seen a doggo like you.'

'Of course you haven't,' says she. 'I am a special doggo. The best,' says she. 'My name is Chee Waa Waa. We are the smallest doggos in the wide world. You may call me Chee if you want.' She blinks her round round eyes at me. 'Chee means power,' says she.

Well there you go. Doggos are a funny lot I do say.

'You are a wild ratty on an adventure. I can see that much,' says Chee. 'But I would love to hear what adventure it is. Why are you running across this city,

Ratty? Where are you going?'

That is a long story. But I am not going anywhere just this minute. So I settle down on the soft floor under the coats and I tell her.

I tell her about Cow and Woolly Woolly Baa Lamb. I tell her about our great journey. I tell her how Minka helped us. 'She was our friend,' says I, 'when we needed one most. Now she needs a friend herself. She is trapped by the Bad Things.'

'So what are you doing about it?' says Chee.

'Well,' says I. 'First I have to find the river and Minka. Then I have to find Greeber's Ground – the City Show is there tomorrow. My friends will be there. When we are all together we must be able to help Minka.'

'Phew!' says Chee, blowing through her yellow nose. 'That sounds a lot to do. For one ratty you know. You need help,' says Chee. 'You need me.'

'I do not think so,' says I. 'One ratty on the run – that is not easy. A ratty and a little yellow dog – that is impossible!'

'Not yellow,' says she. 'Brindled cream.'

'And what about your person?' says I. 'Will she not be worried? You should go back to her.'

'I will go back quite soon, you know,' says Chee. She smiles a wild and wicked smile. 'I am a runny-away sort of doggo I am. She is used to that. I always come home again.'

'I do not need you anyway,' says I crossly. 'I need

my own friends. I want dear Cow and dear Woolly. I need them now!'

'Really?' says Chee. She looks out at the big bright room. 'I do not think a cow and a sheep would help much at this minute. No. You need me!' She turns her round eyes to me. She winks. 'I can get you to the river. And I know Greeber's Ground. My person and I, we go there every year for the Show,' says she.

I leap up onto my four paws. My whiskers shake with joy. Perhaps all is not lost after all. 'Did I hear you right?' says I. 'Did you say you could get me to the river?'

'I thought that might change your mind,' says she. 'Yes, course I can! Just needs cleverness you know!'

'But how? How?' I squeak.

'Well,' says Chee. 'All the roads in this city go over the river. We must find a car or a lorry that is heading that way.' She pauses and tilts her head to one side. 'Course,' says she, 'we might be unlucky. The one we choose may have been over the river already! It's a gamble!' She dances on her four yellow round feet. 'A gamble! Win or lose. Take your chance! That's the way!' She laughs her high doggo laugh as if it's party time and no mistake.

I put my ratty head between my two front paws and I groan. Chee is wild indeed. She is wilder than me by many a rat mile. Then I raise my head. 'All this clever talk is well enough,' says I. 'But how do we get onto a lorry or a car even? We are stuck here you know!'

'Mmmm,' says Chee. 'This shop will have a way in for lorries. We just have to find it.'

'Shop?' I whisper. I do not feel a clever ratty at this moment. I stare around the wide room and all the clothes. 'Shop?'

'Yes. This is a big shop, a store,' says Chee. She tosses her round apple head. 'What did you think it was? It'll have a place where lorries bring things. Sure to. Let us look,' says she. 'Sitting here will not help Minka!'

She is up on her toes. Her eyes flash. She is waiting for off-time. 'Ready?' says she.

Up I leap. I breathe a long deep breath.

'Ready!' says I.

So off we go.

Chasing after Chee is like chasing moonbeams. Quick, zoom one way – behind a door, under a table. Then zip and zap – this way, that, and off again. She runs fast as winking. I am no slowcoach myself. No one sees us. That is what counts.

At last we stop. We tuck behind a box next to a mirror. Chee peers out.

'Oh good!' says she. 'The Toy Department. I always like that best!'

'Chee,' says I. I am breathing hard. I am a plump ratty and running is not my best thing. 'How do you know all about shops and toys and everything?'

'Me?' says Chee. 'A great shopper is my person. Loves places like this. She wouldn't leave me behind, oh no. I tuck into that bag you saw. I peep out when I can. I tell her what suits her. She says shopping with a friend is so much easier.'

But I am listening no longer. I am staring. I am staring at the toys. What a sight! How strange! I see a horse, yes a horse, all speckled and stiff and standing on rockers. And over there I see trains, and cars and buses. But not real size. So tiny and so bright. And each one still as still.

I look up. High over our heads are wires and shapes, dangling like webs, tinkling and shining.

And over there, best of all, I see a mountain pile of soft smiling furred things.

'Who are they?' I ask. It is lovely to see furred friends, but they are so still. Just like the cars and trains. They do not move. They do not speak.

'Those!' says Chee. She laughs. 'Those are cuddly toys,' says she. 'They are meant to look like you and me. Well perhaps not you. I have never seen a ratty toy.'

'Not much like you neither,' says I. 'They have lots of fur and they are jolly-looking.'

'Hmmmm,' says Chee. She peers this way and that. Suddenly she stops. She points with her short yellow nose.

'Look over there, Ratty my friend. That's where we need to be.'

I peer over the bright floor. There on the far side is an open door. Through it I see a little room full of boxes. A man is in the room, pushing the boxes into a square door in the wall.

'Luck, luck!' sings Chee, quiet as can be. 'I am the luckiest doggo ever. That is a lift. A lift for boxes. It will go down to the outside. That's our way out, my friend.'

Yes, there is the lift. I can see it. But right in front of the lift is the man.

And there is another snag. Here in the Toy section there are more people. Big people and little people, men, women and children. How can a ratty and a little yellow doggo get across to that door and past the man?

Chee puts her round head one way and then the other. She looks at me.

'I will cause a stir,' says she. 'I can do that. When I wink, run as quick and quiet as you can. Wait for me in the lift!'

She stands up on her round little paws. She shakes herself.

Then with one great leap she is out in the middle of the floor.

Oh my. Oh my. We are in trouble now. Every face turns towards her.

'Look! Mum!' squeals a little boy.

'Come and look!' yells a little girl.

They all come running. Then they stand looking at

Chee. She is as still as still. As still as all the other animals in the Toy section. As still as the horse on its rocker.

'It's a doggo!' shouts the little boy.

'It is!' shouts the little girl.

'Don't be silly, darling,' says the boy's mother. 'It's not a dog. It's a toy.'

Then Chee starts to move.

How can I explain? I stare and wonder so much that I almost forget to make my run.

First she begins to hum. Hum in a strange kind of whirring hissing way. Hum, buzz, goes she through her shut mouth.

Then she starts to move. First her tail goes. Flick, flack, one way. Flick, flack, the other. Not like a real tail. Strange, stiff, hard. No bending. Flick, flack.

Then she moves her head. But not like Chee at all. She lifts her head. Her neck is straight and stiff. Her eyes stare open. She turns her head sideways and stares one way. Then she turns it again and stares the other way.

This is not Chee, this dog I'm watching. It looks like somebody pretending to be Chee. And not doing so well neither.

'Isn't it clever?' whispers a lady in a green coat. 'How do they do it I wonder!'

Now Chee starts to walk. She lifts a front leg, high like a horse, and sets it down straight ahead. She lifts her back leg and moves that. Then the other front leg. One after the other, high, strutting, like a horse prancing in the deep spring grass.

'Oh, wonderful!' says a man at the back. 'You'd think it was real, wouldn't you?'

'Can I have one?' says the little boy ever so quiet. His eyes are fixed on Chee. He does not blink.

Chee loves all this. I see her eye sparkle.

'Oh Chee my friend,' I mutter under my breath, 'do not get carried away. Remember who we are. Remember the lift.'

She turns sudden and sharp. She spins on her back feet.

'Aaaaaah!' sigh all the people.

Chee's twinkling eye catches mine. She winks. 'Go now,' says her silent mouth at me.

I do.

Off I run, behind the horse and the trains and the tiny cars. Along beside the silent furred ones. Right to the boxroom door. Nobody looks. Nobody sees. Not one little jot. They are all watching Chee.

I'm in the boxroom now – but there is no man here. Where is he? Watching Chee, that's where.

The man's back is towards me. His hands are on his hips.

'I haven't heard of these,' says a lady in front of him.

'New stock,' says he. Then he scratches his head and goes on staring.

In I go. I scuttle across the floor. Up I leap into the hole in the wall. It is a big metal square, dark, shiny.

It is full of boxes, stacked inside each other. I jump inside one.

I turn round. I stand up on my back legs. I peer out. How is Chee going to get here? How can she get away?

She walks round in a big circle, right up close to everyone's toes. They all step back.

'Careful there!' says the man from the boxroom. 'Very valuable toy that is. Special demonstration model that one!'

Chee walks round again, in a bigger circle. Then again.

People are pushing further back now. They step behind the rocking horse. Behind the tiny trains and lorries. Behind the table where the selling lady stands.

Chee jerks her head. Once. Twice. Her round eyes flash.

Then she vanishes.

I see her I do.

But do the people see her, all crowded together and standing on each other's toes?

Do they see her? No they do not.

Chee jumps – that's what she does. She jumps sideways like a grasshopper. One moment she is there. The next she is halfway up the pile of furred friends. Her little yellow face peers out from amongst the yellow bears and the blue rabbits.

There she is. But no one sees her. Except me.

What do the people do? They stir. They mutter. They whisper. They look around them.

'All part of the act,' says the boxroom man. 'Magic stuff eh? Just like the real thing. Wonderful they are. Cheaper to feed than a real dog too.' He laughs loud and long, 'Ho ho ho.'

All the grown-ups laugh too.

'I want a toy dog!' say the little girl and the little boy both together. They rush over to the selling lady. She looks a bit worried.

'Two toy dogs. Yes, of course,' she says. She looks desperately around. She does not know what to do.

Chee winks at me from the high pile of furry faces.

Then quicker than I can blink she dips out of sight. There is one less yellow face in that heap of fur.

I see her creep out against the wall. She skims along behind the toy trains and the lorries and the cars. She dodges in through the boxroom door. In one bound she is up here beside me.

Here is Chee, and me next to her, side by side, in a cardboard box, with our noses sticking over the edge.

'Chee,' says I. 'That was brilliant that was. Brilliant.'

'It was wasn't it?' says Chee. 'I am brilliant. That is a fact and no mistake.' She smiles all over her yellow face. Her little sharp teeth gleam with delight. 'Oh what fun!' says she. 'This is better than sitting in a bag I can tell you.'

'Well,' says I, 'I'm not sure about that. We're sitting in a box now so where's the difference?'

Suddenly clump, clump, clump. Here comes the man on his heavy feet. We huddle down into the bottom of our box. We lie so still that our breath almost stops. We lie so still that a spider comes sliding down the box side and runs over our two backs and never notices that we're not cardboard too. So still.

We are lucky. It is my lucky day and Chee is a lucky doggo. The man does not put more boxes on top of us. Perhaps it has all been too much for him. He needs a sit-down and a rest. So he comes over – we can hear his feet and his breathing. We hear him press a button. We hear doors slide across.

Suddenly, we are jerked downwards so quick that our heads fly up into the air. My whiskers wave above my round ears.

'Oooooooooop!' says I.

'Wheeeeeee!' squeaks Chee. She grins a doggo grin.

Thump! We stop so sudden that my belly hits the bottom of the box with a hard bang.

'Whhhhuuup!' says I. Ratty bellies are round and soft. They are not meant to be walloped against a hard floor.

Chee just leans a little and prances on her curved yellow legs. 'What next?' says she. 'What next?'

The metal doors slide open. Where are we now? What next indeed?

CHAPTER 4

A cold blast of air hits us. Somehow we have come down from the inside of the shop to the outside. We are not at the river yet – but this is one step nearer.

'I was right!' says Chee in my ear. 'Right again, that's me!'

I stick my brown nose over the box edge, slow and careful as can be. I sniff, once, twice. Then I push my ears up and listen. At last I peep over the edge and look.

I am looking out over a concrete yard. It is full of big lorries and small green vans. We are at the top of a ramp. Just below us is a green van. There are two men standing by it.

'Almost time for off,' says the bigger of the two men. He looks at his watch.

'About time too,' says the other. He is a little man and quick. 'I'm ready for my tea.'

'Me too,' says his friend. He looks up. He seems

to stare straight into my ratty eyes. But he has not seen me.

'We could just empty the lift,' says he, 'before we go.'

'Good idea,' says the other. Clump, clump, clump, up the ramp they come. I leap back onto the floor of the box. So does Chee.

'Not much here,' says the little man.

Suddenly – whoops – up into the air we go. The bright sunlight shines down upon us. But the man does not see us. He is holding the box high on his shoulder. I can hear it rustling against his hair.

'Toys!' says he. 'Always such silly shapes these boxes. Mind you these ones are heavier than usual. Perhaps they've forgotten to unpack them!'

He laughs at his own joke. 'Ho ho!' goes he. His friend laughs too.

Chee and I huddle at the bottom of the box.

The man carries the boxes off down the ramp. Lurch, lurch we go. Perhaps I will be sick. I hope not.

'There's not much space left in this van,' says our man. 'I can just about squeeze these in but it'll be a bit of a push.'

Whisk. Thump. Down comes our box onto the edge of the van floor. Then down comes another box on top of us. Down go our heads under it. We are squashed flat against the cardboard.

The man pushes. He is going to get these last boxes

in somehow. He pushes harder. My nose and whiskers are crushed up against the box side.

I have not heard a squeak from Chee since we were picked up. She is squashed as flat as me. That is not good news. A doggo should not be as flat as a ratty. Chee is a little doggo but she is twice as big as me. Or she was before she was squashed at the bottom of this box.

I can feel her sides going in and out. She is still breathing. If any doggo will get out of this safe and sound, Chee will. That is what I hope.

One more push, one more heave. The man has got us wedged in.

'That's it!' he says. 'Not a whisker more space in there!'

What does he know about whiskers I'd like to know? My whiskers will never be the same after all this squashing.

'Heave ho, Mike!' he calls out. 'We need a hand with these doors!'

Clump, clump, a third man comes up. We hear his feet against the hard ground. Together they push the doors shut. The boxes shift even closer together.

'Are you taking this van out?' says our man to Mike.

'Yeh, I'll be off now!' says Mike. 'Tarrah!' says he.

We hear him march round to the driver's door. He climbs in. He slams the door and settles himself. Then he starts the engine.

'What an adventure!' says Chee in my ear.

Her voice is sort of flattened, sort of squashed. It is a voice with no air in it. But it is Chee's voice right enough. My heart goes pitapat with joy.

'Oh Chee,' says I. 'You are well. You can speak. We are both here and in our fur and on our way!'

'On our way, yes indeed,' says Chee in her squashed voice, 'but where to?'

Then she begins to struggle.

I have said that doggos are bigger than ratties, even when they are little doggos. They are stronger too. Chee's little legs are tough as Farmer's stout stick. They are strong as Pig's snout when he digs in the ground for acorns. She pushes her four feet down, and down again.

'Help me!' she says. Her teeth are clenched together I can hear. 'Help me, Ratty. Heave for your life.'

So I do. I square my short legs onto the cardboard floor. I tense my furry shoulders. I tuck my head in and fold my ears against my neck.

'Now!' she calls out. 'Heave!'

She heaves. I heave. We heave again.

The man has pushed the boxes hard into place but we push harder. Up goes the box which lies upon our backs. We press it up against the van roof. The box folds up. It flattens. It slides off sideways.

Up go our heads. We peer out over the box edge.

What do we see? The van is crammed with boxes. But there is light. High up along each van side are little square windows.

'The bridge isn't far from the shop – I know that,' whispers Chee. 'My person and me have walked there lots of times. We may be close to the river already – if we are going in the right direction! If we are going in the wrong direction, we have to get out as soon as possible! And start again!'

I put my furry head between my little front paws. 'I do not want to start again,' says I.

The van stops suddenly. All the boxes sway and shake.

Chee peers up through the windows.

'That could be a red light over there,' says Chee. 'Perhaps we have stopped at the bridge lights.'

'If it is the bridge,' I whisper, 'how can we get out of here?'

Chee turns her yellow head towards me. She winks one round eye. She smiles.

Then she lifts her golden nose until it is pointing straight up towards the low roof of the van. She opens her mouth – and she howls.

Howls I say. But howl is not the right word.

I have heard doggos howl, many a time. They howl when the moon is full overhead. They howl when they fancy they are wild wolves in the snow, in the time when doggos ran free, and people feared them. Howling is howling. It is a round sort of noise, long and soft at the edges and floating. That is not what Chee is doing.

She screams. She cries. She sobs. She wails. The noise is so high and piercing that my ratty ears throb.

'Oooooooh! Aaaaaah!' she screams. 'Eeeeee!'

Higher and higher. Louder and louder.

'What's that!' yells Mike from the other side of the glass. 'What is that? Who is that?'

'Eeeeeeeeh!' sings out Chee. The van sides hum and quiver from one end to the other. The sound goes straight through my furry body like a sharp tooth. It echoes back and forwards from roof to side to door and back again.

'My goodness me!' yells Mike. 'Someone is being killed inside my van! Help! Murder!' shouts Mike.

We hear him throw open his door. He leaps out onto the road.

'Help! Murder!' he yells again.

The red light is green now. Mike does not care. We hear him run round to the back of the van. We hear people shout. One person screams, a bit like Chee but not so loud.

'Murder? Who? Where?' There are voices on all sides. 'What is it? Who is hurt?'

And then another voice. 'You can't stop here, sir. No you can't. You're holding up the traffic.'

42

'Oh,' says Chee with a smile all over her yellow face. 'Oh lovely. A policeman!'

She tilts her head back and starts all over again.

'Officer!' says Mike. 'Listen to that. Hear that! Someone is dying in my van. Help me!' says Mike.

'I see what you mean,' says the policeman. 'Get those doors open!'

Mike does. Click, once, twice. The doors snap open. They swing wide.

All the boxes, crammed so tight, squashed so close, start to move. They stretch, they breathe out. All together. They push apart, and off they go. They bounce, they pour. Out through the open van doors. A cardboard river, a box cascade, out onto the hard road.

Well that is that. Boxes everywhere. Cars stopped. People standing up to their knees in cardboard. Lights changing, green, yellow, red. Red, yellow, green. Nothing going anywhere.

The policeman is not happy.

'Where is that poor screaming soul?' says Mike. 'Where is the person who is hurt?'

Then he sees Chee standing on the van floor. I pull back and hide in the dark shadows at the back of the van. This is not a safe place for me.

Chee steps forward into the middle of the floor. She gives one more little scream – just to show that she is the screamer. Mike stares. His eyes go round like little moons from surprise. Then Chee wags her tail. She smiles her doggo smile. She leaps into Mike's arms.

'My goodness me,' says Mike. 'Am I dreaming?'

Chee lifts her nose and licks his face. 'I am not dreaming,' says Mike.

'No, you are not dreaming,' says the policeman, 'but I wish I was. That looks a valuable dog to me.'

'Precious is the word!' says Chee but of course no one understands her.

'I'd get it back to its owner double quick if I was you,' says the policeman. 'I'd take it myself but I've got a bit of bother to sort out here as you may have noticed.'

He takes a phone out of his pocket. I hope you know what phones are. People love them. They talk to them all the time and take them everywhere. Anyway now this policeman takes out his phone and talks to it for a little while. Then he starts talking to the crowd.

'Move along there,' he says. 'Nobody is hurt. Nobody is murdered. It is just a little dog.'

They don't move along at all. 'A dog!' they say, 'where? Oh how sweet!'

Everyone wants to see Chee in Mike's arms. People are taking photographs. Mike is smiling. Chee is wagging her tail. She looks as cheerful as can be.

I am still hiding in the dark van. I am not sure what to do next.

Then Chee sings out in her high doggo voice, 'Friend Ratty, the river is here. I see it. Bright and flowing just below us. I shall make these people move. Then you must run for it.'

I begin to move forward slowly and carefully. She turns her eyes towards me. She flashes her pointed white teeth in a happy smile.

'I shall see you again you can be sure,' she calls out to me.

'What a funny noise that dog makes,' says one person. 'It is almost like talking.'

Chee winks her eye. She calls out to me again in her high clear voice.

'I must go now,' says she. 'This nice man will take me home. But I will seek you out, brother Ratty, hero Ratty. Tomorrow,' calls she, 'I shall get to the City Show. To Greeber's Ground. I will, I will,' she yaps. 'Remember! I shall look for you there!'

'Be safe!' she calls out. Then she leaps down from Mike's arms.

'Ooooh!' sighs the crowd. Chee does not go far. She runs a few steps. Then she leaps up again, onto the front of one of the cars. The people follow her.

She has made a safe space for me. Out I leap. Out of that dark space onto the hard road. I dash through the people feet. I run between two car wheels.

In front of me is a sort of stone fence.

Through I go. And then I stop.

I stop sudden and quick because there is nowhere else to run. I am on the high edge of the bridge here. Far below me is the river, cold and wet and gleaming. It is dark and flecked with green.

But not brown. I must find the brown stream. Where can it be?

I peer over the river to the far side. I see a high river wall along the water's edge. Beyond the wall there is a river walk. People scuttle along it to and fro. Above the people stand high buildings, old buildings. One says MUSEUM in big white letters. The next one says THEATRE in lights that glow and blink. These are new words. I do not know what they mean. But I am sure they do not mean anything about streams and water so they are no help to me. That is sure.

I perch there. I watch the river and I wonder. There is a rush of feathers over my head. A pale bird flaps down towards the water. I watch it as it flies. It floats up on the breeze, then down again. It skims sideways. It folds its wings and drops lightly down upon the soft sand on the far side of the river.

On the far side of the river. By the water's edge. In front of the river wall.

And suddenly I see, behind the bird, a round hole in the wall.

I stare. And then I stare again.

Out of that hole flows water. Out of that dark hole and over the bright sand into the river.

Brown water.

'It is the brown stream,' I whisper to myself on my high perch. 'Over there. On that far bank. I have found the brown stream. Oh Minka, hold on. Hold on. I will be with you soon.'

Off I run, hard and fast, along my narrow rat ledge over the river to the brown stream and to Minka.

CHAPTER 5

The bright sun begins to drop in the sky. It will soon be evening. Dark shadows fill every corner.

I reach the bridge end and down I leap onto a wall. Then down again into the dark corner of the river walk. People walk by, talking, laughing. No one sees me.

I take a breath and scuttle to the edge of the walkway. Over I go. Down onto the soft wet sand of the river edge.

The river is moving fast. Little waves lap near me as I bound along. I see ahead of me the brown smudge of the stream where it crosses the sand. Three more leaps and I am there.

Right above me now, in the river wall, is the great round hole. From its metal mouth trickles the stream water.

I stand up tall on my back legs. I reach up and

grasp the metal edge with my two front paws. I stare into the dark. I smell the cold air. It smells of bones, and fur, and blood and fear. This is no place for a ratty who likes to be comfortable and safe. That is what I think.

'If you're going in there mate, say goodbye to your friends!' says a piping voice shrill in my ear.

I spin round so fast that I tumble down onto the sand. Then I jump up quick as quick. A ratty should not be caught out like this. Ratties should be watchful at all times. That is what my mother said and right she was. Watchful or dead is what she said. I am glad I am still breathing.

It is the little bird, here in front of me. He puts his head on one side. He peers at me with his bright eye.

'Surprised you did I?' says he. 'Bigger surprise in there I'm telling you!' He laughs. A long shaking laugh that goes from high to low. Then he closes his sharp beak and stares at me again.

He is little and pale and mottled. But he is tall. His legs are so long that he looks as if he was perching on stilts. His legs are the colour of old blood.

'Like them do you?' says he, waving a leg in

my direction. He dances a bit on the sand. 'Red as blood they be,' he sings. 'But let's not talk of blood round here. No, sir. No indeed!'

'What do you mean?' I whisper. I do not like the sound of this.

Bird does not reply. He just dances a bit more and stares back at me over his long beak.

'My friend is in that tunnel,' says I.

'Your friend?' says the bird.

He stops dancing and stands very still. His pointed bird face fills with sadness. 'Your friend?' he says. 'Oh Ratty, stranger rat, I am sorry.'

There is a little silence. The river washes by. I hear people feet clump clumping over my head but no one looks over the wall.

'I have to find her,' I say.

He nods his long beak. He says nothing. I turn and scramble up into the tunnel mouth. I take a step forward into the gloom.

Then from behind me I hear his high voice calling. 'I shall watch for you,' says he. 'I will call out if danger comes this way. You will hear me however deep you go. Find her safe!' he calls out. But he does not sound so sure about it I must say.

I turn and leap away. Into that dark tunnel. His twittering cry echoes round me from the curved metal walls.

I gallop on.

I see now that I am in a huge metal pipe, a drain.

Huge and old. The brown water flows slowly along the bottom. On each side of the water there is a muddy line of dead leaves, and twigs, and people rubbish. My feet splash soft as I run. Above my head the metal pipe gleams.

I run on. But something has changed. My feet crunch now. I stop. I look down. It is dark but ratty eyes are used to that. By my feet is a white gleam. I look again. I sniff.

Bones. I am walking on bones. Tiny broken bones.

They are snapped so fine that they make a spiky white sand under my feet. It is like the bed that Fox Friend lies on in the cold spring, when her cubs are new.

My fur stands stiff on my back. I sweat with fear. Who lives here? Do they eat ratties? I see no rat bones here. Mice bones yes. Bird bones yes. Shells of sea things, fish bones. No rat bones. Not yet.

I sweat and pant but on I must go. Leap, crunch. Leap, crunch. On I go. Into the dark.

It is heavy dark now, so far from the river. High above my head through the hard earth I can hear the sound of cars and buses and people, far off.

I pause.

Something has moved.

Before I have time to think, a strong paw seizes my tail. I am off my feet in one jerk. I dangle upside down in the dark. Above me two eyes glow red as rubies.

Upside down. In the dark. Hanging like a bat – or like a dead thing on Farmer's fence. That is not a happy thought.

I wriggle. I struggle. It is no use. The hard paw grips my tail. I am an upside-down ratty with nowhere to go.

'Oh ratkin,' says a voice so deep so harsh so sad. 'Oh ratkin, how brave you are. And how foolish.'

My heart pounds in my chest. I squeak with fright. I open my mouth to squeak again. I take a deep breath. That is a mistake. My nose is just above the water. I breathe in water! My nose fills with cold and wetness. Uuuugh!

So then I sneeze and cough as if I am going to burst.

This will not do Ratty, I say to myself, as soon as I can breathe again. A ratty has his pride.

I take a slow and easy breath. I speak as calm as I

am able, upside down though I be. 'Who are you?' says I. My voice shakes only a little bit.

All I can see is dark fur and two red red eyes. This must be the one who makes the bones under my feet. Bone-cruncher his very self. He dangles me by my tail as if I was no weight at all. And as you know I am a round and well-fed ratty.

'I wonder?' says he at last. 'I wonder? Could you be her friend?'

Her friend? Her? Can he mean Minka?

I give a great twist. I try to leap free. I go nowhere. His paw clenches my tail as tight as tight.

So I ask again, 'Who are you? What is your name?'

His hand on my tail grips even tighter for a second. I hear him shake his head. His voice comes down to me, cross and sharp. 'Name?' he says. 'Name? What do you mean? Name?'

This is very odd I must say. It is even odder when you are upside down, unless you are a bat of course, which I am not.

'What do your friends call you?' I say. 'How do you know they mean you?'

'Oh,' he says. 'What do they call me? I see. I'm Number 29. Cage 29. That's me.' He sounds pleased to understand. 'So that is what you call a name. I will remember,' says he. 'Yes, my name is 29. Row A you know. A29 if you want the whole thing. It is one of the top numbers as you see,' says he.

Twenty-nine! So this is 29. This is the creature that I

am to fear. And he holds me by my tail over the white-bone sand. Not good news you must agree. My heart skips a beat or two. 'You are in trouble Rattyo,' I whisper in my head. 'What a lot and lot of trouble you are in!'

I take a deep breath. 'Put me down,' I say. I sound as bold as brass but my ratty heart is failing me. 'Put me down onto my four feet.'

'All right,' says he. 'But you won't get far on those four feet. No indeed. You will come with me. I want her to see you.'

'Her?' I say. 'Who is her?'

'My friend,' says he. 'My friend. She is safe and well and in the best of prisons. But she does not seem happy. She talks of a ratty. She wants to see him. And,' says he, 'I think that you may be the ratty she means!'

His hand lowers slowly. He sets me down upon my feet on the stream verge. But he grips my tail as hard as ever.

'Ahead!' says he. 'Go that way. You can run as fast as you can go. There is no way out. No way out!'

His chuckle follows me as I dart forward up the tunnel into the dark.

I run. Round one bend, then another.

My nose hits a wire mesh.

I smash into it. I tumble back into the wet crunchy sand. He is right. The mesh blocks the whole tunnel, from roof to floor, from one side to the other. Mesh, old wire mesh, thick with dead leaves, and rubbish, and paper and all the things people drop. The brown stream seeps through it but ratties are not water drops. I hear 29's splashing feet bound up behind me.

'That way,' he hisses. I turn my head and see. Above us is a gap, a smaller pipe into the roof. 'Up there,' says he.

Up I go. I have no choice.

Up I leap and off along this new pipe. It leads steep uphill. It is a tight fit for 29 but that does not bother him.

Suddenly my head hits something hard. A stone roof. I look this way and that to find my way. To one side I see a gap, a crack between stone and ground. The mud is beaten flat by many feet. Beyond the crack I see a dull light. I smell dust and cold.

There is only one way so through I go. Then I stop.

I am dreaming – that is what I think.

It is grey and dusty and dim. Bit by bit my eyes make it out. Bit by bit.

Dreaming I am. Dreaming I must be. Dreaming of old things, and broken things. Of swords and guns, of chests and books, of robes and great feathered hats.

I am in a high chill room. The walls are made of heavy blocks of old stone. In this room is piled every kind of thing that you can think of. Every kind of ancient thing.

Next to my paws lies a glove, crusted with jewels and the thumb torn off. Beyond is an old chest, hanging with spiders' webs. On top of the chest lies a dusty feathered hat that mice have chewed.

In the corner is a metal man – that is what I think at first. Then I see it is a metal suit to fit a man. One metal leg is missing so that he leans against the wall.

'Where is this?' I whisper. I fear the place. Old things can be cruel if they are left too long.

'This is the Museum,' says 29.

He is behind me. He has pushed his way up through the narrow gap. 'The Museum. It is the store-room of the Museum. This end of it is full of broken things. No one comes here. Upstairs we hear feet, lots of feet. But no one comes here.

'Except us,' he says. And he chuckles.

I turn to look at him. It is the first time I have seen him whole and in the light. I stare. And stare again.

This is Number 29. Cruncher of bones. Terror of white hens. The baddest of bad things as I fear.

He is a mink. Like Minka. But so big. Twice as big as dear Minka, and paler. His fur is long and thick. It is soft as longest meadow grass. It is the colour of fallen leaves, speckled with frost. It shines and glints and rustles as he moves.

He sees me staring. He looks down at his fur. There is a strange look on his face.

'I grow the fur they like to wear,' says he. 'I am the top grade. That's me! The very best.'

His voice is proud but his eyes are blank and sad.

He is the most beautiful creature that ever ratty saw in this wide world. So beautiful he is. But his eyes are blank as a frozen river.

'Oh no,' I whisper to myself. 'Oh no.'

He is far away in his head. That I can see. He is a lost thing.

And I am in his power. But I must not despair. Not yet.

Then a muffled scratching sound catches my

round ears. I listen. I step forward. I listen again. I scuttle round the old chest. I creep past a high pile of ancient books.

And there she is. Minka.

CHAPTER 6

'Minka!' I cry. 'Oh Minka, dear friend. But how cruel, how cruel.'

For here is Minka, alive, breathing, leaping, crying. But she is muffled. Silenced. Between her and me is glass. Thick glass.

Minka is inside a glass box, a big glass box. The box is perched high on a golden table.

The glass is as thick as winter ice. She is striking at the glass with her paws. She is calling to me. But all I hear is a whimper as if from far away.

'Bars are best. Of course,' says 29 behind me. 'Nothing can beat bars. She would like bars better I am sure. But she is happy with the glass. I think. Almost. For the time being. That glass case had a King's crown in it once. Now she has it. She must be pleased at that.'

'Pleased!' I say. 'Happy!'

I stare at Minka's desperate face. Her pointed muzzle cries and calls to me through the glass.

'Well,' says 29. 'No one likes a cage at first you know. But cages are best. I know that now. We all love them in the end. Free is frightening, you will agree.'

He waves his paw at Minka. 'I put her there to keep her safe,' says he. 'Not out on that wild river. Poor thing – that's where I found her. Wild and free. Poor thing! Of course it is different for me. I cannot hide away. I have a job to do. But at least she can be shut up safe.'

He frowns and tugs at one dark furred ear. His eyes are puzzled. 'You know,' says he, 'I do not think she is as happy as she could be. I do not understand it. Something is wrong.'

He shakes his head as if there was a pain inside it. He lifts his troubled eyes. He sees Minka and smiles to see her. But she has covered her face with her paws. Tears slide down her shining fur.

29 watches the tears. Again he frowns. Again he tugs at one dark ear. 'Have I got something wrong?' he mutters. 'How can that be?'

He frowns. The pain gleams in his eyes.

Then all at once, far off, comes a high sweet sound. It echoes through the tunnels. It reaches us even here, high and clear. It is the red-legged bird. He calls for me.

'Danger!' I say in my heart.

29 is listening too. He sniffs the air. He turns his head. He hears something. I hear it too. The scamper

of many paws. The scratch of claws. The panting breath of many hot mouths.

'They are here,' says he.

He turns quickly. 'Key!' he shouts in his harsh voice.

Out from under an old chest scuttles a grey mouse. Tiny, round. The mouse does not look at me. She does not look at Minka. She bobs her head to 29. In her hands she carries a tiny golden key.

'Now!' says 29.

The mouse leaps up onto a dusty chair. She scuttles over the faded arms and jumps to the table top. She runs up to the glass box. I see there is a lock in the metal base at one side.

Mouse struggles with the key. She lifts it up onto her tiny shoulder. She pushes it into the lock. Then she jumps round. Once, twice, three times. There is a click. The whole side of the glass box swings open on its hinges.

29 grabs me round my furry neck. His massive paw lifts me up. In a moment I am on the high table.

'In you go,' says 29.

He shoves me in.

Into the glass prison.

Then slam, snap, goes the glass door. Click, click goes the golden key. And we are here together, Minka and I. Stuck in glass like fish in ice.

Minka reaches forward. She hugs me with her furred arms. Then she turns and stares and so do I.

Even through the glass we hear it. The thudding sound of many voices and many feet. We listen.

It is a marching beat, a marching song. A song of two words, beating on and on.

'Fear us! Fear us! Fear us!'

A dreadful song. Loud and savage. It throbs towards us through the air and through the ground.

'Fear us! Fear us! Fear us!'

Minka stares at me. Her eyes are wide with fright.

What is this sound? What is this song?

I see a crack in the glass. A thin and crooked crack just above our heads. I stretch up and press my ear to it. I hear clearer than before.

The noise fills the air around us. They are here!

Up they come through the floor, here, and there, and here again, from holes and tunnels on every side. They come.

Animals. Creatures like you and me. They chant. They sing. They laugh. They bare their fierce fangs. From every side they climb up through the stone floor. Into this high and dusty room.

Rats. There are rats there. I am ashamed to say it. And cats too. Thin cats with bones that stand up through their fur. And two fat cats with the fur rolled thick round plump cruel necks. Two white ferrets bound up out of the floor. Their pink eyes shine and flash. And here come four lean and short-legged dogs with savage faces.

'They are the Bad Things,' says Minka softly.

'But where have they come from?' I whisper.

'The riverside,' says she. 'They are all the bad things of the riverside. They were bad before but they had no plan or leader. They stole what they could. They killed where they could. That tunnel has been full of death this long time.'

I shudder. I remember the white bones under my paws.

'Now they have bigger work,' says Minka. '29 came. He found them. Now they follow him.'

'But what is he doing?' says I. 'He says he has a job to do. What does he mean? What does he want?'

'He wants revenge,' says Minka. She turns her dark pebble eyes towards me.

'I do not understand,' I say. 'Revenge for what?'

'He has spent his life on a fur farm,' she whispers. Her eyes are far away and full of sadness.

'Please tell me,' I say. 'Please. I do not know what a fur farm is.'

'A fur farm,' says Minka, 'is a place for creatures like him and me. Wild things with thick soft coats. They keep us in cages. When we grow big, they kill us. They sell our fur to make coats for people.'

I shake my head. It sounds so strange. But 29 is proof of it. Some dreadful thing has hurt his heart, that is for sure.

'He was born on the fur farm,' says Minka. 'I was born free you know. It is different. But 29 grew up there. They kept him alive a long time, longer than all his friends. They wanted his fur for a special coat, you see. And then some people came and opened all the doors and out he ran. Now he wants revenge. Revenge for his dead friends. Revenge for his fright. For fearing the end day after day. For all that.'

I look out at the dancing, prancing shapes that fill the dim room. Cold fills my heart.

'What is his plan?' I ask after a while.

'He cannot kill people,' she says, 'they are too big. So he will kill their pets. He can't do it on his own. That is why he leads these Bad Things.'

I shake my head. This is not how creatures fight. Revenge is people talk. 'Oh Minka,' says I. 'This is people badness. They have turned his mind.'

'Yes,' says she. 'He is mad in his head. He does not know what he is doing. What have pets done to him? It is not sensible you know.'

She looks past me. I turn round. There is a new movement outside the glass. Something is happening. I peer out.

The creatures are moving and settling. They turn and crouch down into a long half-circle.

Their eyes gleam so bright that they do not look like creatures of ordinary breath and fur. They are more like the things that come in bad dreams.

29 moves forward. He takes his place at the head of the long circle. He sits back. He looks at each one of the panting leering faces.

He begins to speak. So quiet is his voice that I must lean my ear to the crack to catch his words.

'Fear,' says he. 'We will bring fear.'

The creatures nod. Their eyes gleam. They say nothing.

'The people will fear,' says 29. 'They will look for their pets. They will search. But their pets will be gone.' He looks around that grim circle.

'All their pets gone. Lost,' says he. 'Who will do this?' He sings out the words in a high strange voice.

'We will!' The creatures shout back at him in a sudden great roar. The glass shakes against my listening ear.

'And the pets. They will be frightened to step outside. They will fear the rustle in the hedge. The shadow by the gate. Who will make them fear?'

'We will!' The sound is softer this time and grim.

'The people will cry. There will be tears upon their faces. Who will make them cry?'

'We will!' they roar out, loud once more, into the high darkness.

29 lifts his sharp muzzle to the dark roof far above. Then he laughs.

Tears rise to my eyes – and that is not a common thing with my people. 29 is a mad thing, I say. A broken thing. And now he wants to break others.

I cover my eyes with my paws. I hide my thoughts in darkness. I do not want to see.

But Minka gives me a nudge. I look up again.

The Bad Things are quiet now. 29 is talking in a low voice. I press my ear against the crack to hear him.

'Greeber's Ground,' says 29. 'That is the Big One. We start there. The City Show on Greeber's Ground. Our time. Our revenge,' says he. 'Greeber's Ground will pay.

'A first payment,' says he.

I jump up and down behind the glass. 'Greeber's Ground!' I hiss. 'Greeber's Ground!'

'What is Greeber's Ground?' says Minka. 'What a strange name. What does it mean?'

'Greeber's Ground is in the City,' says I. 'There is a Show there tomorrow. I know it because Cow will be there. And Woolly. And half the pets in the City!'

'Oh no!' says Minka. Her face is full of fear. 'Pets. All together in one place. That will be his chance.'

I look back at her. She is right. That is his plan. Fear rises in my heart.

But I think again. 'Yes,' says I, 'but Woolly and Cow will be there. And Chee too. You have not met Chee but she is a good friend in a tight place as I know well. We will have our friends to help us.'

Then we hear 29 again. I turn back to the glass.

'Tomorrow,' says 29. 'That is the time. Tomorrow. So tonight – let us have a little trip along the river. A river raid,' says he. 'We will pick up something no doubt. And have a snack or two. Before the big day!'

Every wicked mouth laughs its wicked laugh. They

begin to move. I see no signal but they rise upon their soft and clawed feet. They stretch. They shake.

They start to circle.

It is a dance, almost. A song, almost.

They weave here and there across that dusty floor. They dance in a long line. They wave their paws and tails. They snarl with their sharp and yellow teeth. They chant as they go. Quiet at first. Then louder. And louder still. They sing out.

> *'We will bite,*
> *We'll tear, we'll chew,*
> *Fear us, you pets,*
> *And people too,*
> *FEAR US!'*

It has no sense or so I think. Yet they sing on. Their wicked eyes glow.

> *'We will bite,*
> *We'll tear, we'll chew,*
> *Fear us, you pets,*
> *And people too,*
> *FEAR US!'*

I watch them dance and shout and sing. My blood runs cold inside my ratty heart.

29 rises to his four feet. He stretches his long and beautiful body. His fur ripples and glows in the faint

light. He lifts his head and sniffs. Then he bares his sharp teeth.

'I will have my revenge,' says he.

He turns with a bounding leap. He waves his tail in a great arc of shining fur. He leaps away and disappears with a quick flicker down under the stone slab.

There is a roar from all the Bad Things. 'We go!' they shout together.

After him they pour. In a flashing river of fur and tail and whiskers. Under that cold slab. Down through that dark tunnel. They are gone and we are here alone.

Minka stares at me. I stare back.

Then I shake myself. It is no good being frightened. 'This is all madness and badness,' says I. 'We must stop them. We must stop the Bad Things.'

CHAPTER 7

'We must stop them.' That is what I say. It is easy to sound brave. But I am not feeling brave. I am shaking all over.

One day, when I was a very small ratty indeed, I ate so much cheese that my belly almost popped. I had bad dreams that night. Very bad. But nothing so bad as what I have seen now.

'It is nightmare time,' says I. 'It is all mad badness and we must stop it.'

'Yes, yes,' says Minka. 'But how?'

I try to think. It is not easy.

'First we must get out of here,' says I. 'Then we must find my friends. We cannot do this on our own. All of us together must stop the Bad Things.'

'But how can we get out of here?' says Minka again.

I do not know. That is the truth.

'There is no way,' says she. 'The glass is cracked but

it is a narrow crack and we cannot make it wider. The door is locked. This metal base is strong. 29 knows that we cannot get out.'

As she speaks I see a movement on the floor below. A little grey movement. The mouse. The very mouse who locked us in.

Then I look again.

The mouse is staring up at me. Then she starts to move. She brings her two little front paws together. She bunches up her tail and sits back. Then she starts to sway. She sways one way. Then she sways another. I stare.

Minka has noticed me staring. 'What is the matter?' she asks.

Then she sees the mouse too.

Mouse starts to sway again. One way, then the other. She rocks so hard that at last she tumbles, flat upon the hard floor. Then up she jumps.

I run forward and press my nose to the glass. 'I think I understand!' I cry.

Mouse is staring up at me. She points below us to somewhere near the floor. I peer down to where her grey paw points.

'I do! I understand!' I cry. 'I see!'

Mouse is smiling now all over her whiskered mousy face. She can see that I understand.

'What? What?' asks Minka. 'Tell me!'

'This table is broken – that is what Mouse is telling us. One leg is cracked. Mouse means that we must make the glass box sway. If we make it rock, the table will tumble over! And us with it! She does not dare unlock us,' says I, ' but she has shown us what to do. We must bounce against these glass sides until the table leg breaks.'

'Yes! Yes!' cries Minka. 'I see!'

'Thank you, Mouse,' I whisper through the glass. 'Now we know what we must do.'

Minka begins at once. She leaps high into the air and crashes up against the glass wall. Thump goes her body. Down she tumbles. Then she leaps again. To the other side.

Up I jump too. I have short legs but I am fat. As I hit the glass I feel the table sway. Just a bit, just a little bit. Minka feels it too.

'Together,' she says, 'let us work together.'

So together we leap. Together we hit the glass wall. The glass groans. The table leans a little. We fall back together onto our metal cage floor. We look at each other. We smile.

'We will do this,' says Minka through her white teeth.

'We will,' says I.

Off we go again.

It takes a while. It takes a long while. We leap. We hit the glass. We fall. Each time we hit the glass, the table sways further.

'Now! One last time!' cries Minka.

She hurls herself upwards higher than ever. And I am after her. My little back legs coil and thrust. Up I go, a ratty cannon ball. We hit the glass together. We feel the table tilt and rock. We feel it reach the balancing point.

We feel it go.

Crack! The table leg snaps .

Whoosh! The glass box slides across the dusty table top.

Smash! It hits the stone floor.

The glass top flies one way. The metal base falls the other.

We are free.

Free.

We stand on the dusty floor and look about us. Mouse is here right in front of us.

'Thank you,' I say. 'Dear Mouse, a thousand times thank you.'

Mouse nods her grey head sadly. 'Yes,' says she. 'This time I did right. But most times I look away when bad things happen.' She is so glum that all her fur hangs grey and dull around her. 'I am not brave,' says she.

'You have freed us and that is brave enough,' says I. 'You have been good to us. What is your name?'

She straightens up. A proud gleam comes in her eye. 'I am a heritage mouse,' says she. 'All this is heritage, you know.' She points around her in the dusty space. 'That means mouses too I must suppose.'

'Of course,' I say. A heritage mouse is new to me. 'Why not?'

'You are not safe even now,' says Heritage. 'You must be far away before the Bad Things come back. They will be out until dawn light but then they will return.'

'Which way can we go?' I ask. 'We must get to Greeber's Ground. Our friends are there. And soon the Bad Things will be there too!'

'Oh I know Greeber's Ground,' says Heritage. 'Of course I do. It is a big green place. People walk on it. And take their dogs. And fly kites. And leave bits of food for mice like me. It is not far.'

'How do we get there?' I ask.

'Under that far corner there,' says she, 'you'll find a pipe and then a drain. Follow the drain uphill until you smell grass.'

I sigh. I haven't smelled grass for a long time. It will be nice.

'Will you be safe?' asks Minka looking at Mouse. 'Will 29 punish you when he gets back?'

'I must pretend to be a prisoner,' says Heritage. 'Push me in the high drawer in that chest, there where the key is kept. I'll be comfy there. Then 29 will think I fought you!'

So we do as she says. I pull open the drawer with my paws. Mouse leaps in. 'Do not worry over me,' says she. 'I can squeeze out of the back here if he is late.' Minka smiles and sets her shoulder to the drawer. Click shut it goes.

'Goodbye,' says a tiny voice from inside the great chest. 'Goodbye.'

We are already on our way. We run to the corner by the wall. Down a dark pipe we go. And here below us we see a trickle of dirty water in a round drain.

Uphill – that is what Mouse said. We watch which way the water runs. Then uphill we go.

We splash along. The bottom of the drain is wet and it is dirty. Soon my brown coat is sticky with mud. My whiskers are wrapped in cobwebs and dead flies.

I sneeze and cough. The dirt is getting in my throat.

Minka looks back at me in the half-light. She ruffles up her fur in angry spikes. She snarls and hisses through her sharp teeth.

'This is a vile and ratty place!' she snarls. 'We minks

need clear skies and clear water. Oh horrid place! Oh dirty ratty place! How could you bring us here!'

Now this is not polite I think. Not kind nor friendly neither. I open my mouth to argue.

Then suddenly I see a dim chink of light. Just ahead of us.

The sweet smell of grass floats to our noses.

'At last!' says Minka. Her eyes shine. She leaps forward along the drain.

I leap after her. 'Stop! Stop!' I cry. I catch up with her. 'We must be careful,' says I. 'It is not quite dark yet. There may be people about. Let us look carefully before we climb out.'

The light comes from a broken grating. I peer out.

The drain comes out in the side of a ditch. The day is fading now. But there is light enough to see a fence, straight in front of us. Beyond the fence are trucks and tents and huts.

I peer this way and that. 'I see no person here,' says I. I look again. I hear distant voices near the trucks. 'I think that must be the Show Ground,' says I. 'If we go carefully we should be safe.'

So we slide out through the broken grating. Into the ditch.

There is still no one in sight.

'I have had enough of creeping in ditches and drains!' cries Minka. 'Come on!'

Out she bounds onto the open grass and me after her. We run through the half-light towards the fence.

'Look there,' says Minka.

On two white poles above our heads is a notice.

Furry Pets and Farm Friends.
Your City Show
Come one, Come all to Greeber's Ground
A Family Day Out!

'I think that is the same notice that Hat Man was putting up,' says I. 'It says something about a Show. Do you know, Minka, I do not know what a Show is.'

'It is no good asking me,' says Minka. 'There are no Shows on the wild riverside.'

So we stare at the notice and wonder. Chee would know. Chee knows everything. But Chee is not here.

'Come on,' says I. 'Let us find Cow and Woolly.'

Under the fence we slide.

There are big tents everywhere. They gleam white in the evening gloom. Some are lit up. Some are dark and full of shadows.

'If Cow and Woolly Woolly Baa Lamb are here,' says I, 'they will be eating, you can be sure. It is their teatime now and night is on its way.'

'We must look where the lights are then,' says Minka.

Just then I hear it. Not so far away. Floating through the dark air.

'Baaaa' and 'Baaaa' again. It is Woolly. I am certain of it.

Then a long rising 'Moooooooo'. Not so loud but floating out towards us. Calling us.

'Oh joy!' I cry. 'Cow and Woolly. Both here. And waiting for us.'

I leap forward past the tents and ropes and buckets and feedbags and all the things that block our way. I scramble forward to the bright side of a small tent to one side of the path. I hear Minka panting just behind me.

I stick my nose under the canvas tent wall. I look into the bright warm space. I look into Cow's kind eyes and Woolly's fierce face.

'Dear Ratty,' says Cow. 'We hoped and hoped you would get here. And now you are. Welcome, dear friend. How glad I am to see you safe.'

'Ratty!' snorts Woolly. 'Here and just in time for tea! I am glad you are safe. And who is that behind you?'

Minka has stuck her pointed face under the canvas. She blinks her pebble eyes. She smiles so wide that I see every white tooth in her sharp jaw.

'Dearest of friends,' she cries. 'Dear Cow. Dear Woolly. How long it is since I saw you last. And now you are here to help me and to help us all.' She bounces in a little circle in her joy.

Cow begins to dance too on her four big feet. 'Minka!' she cries. 'Oh Minka, safe and sound! You are well and you are free! How good that is!'

Her eyes sparkle. She shakes her big black and white head. She pushes her curvy horns into the tent roof and blows out through her big soft mouth.

Then she stops still and peers down at us. 'Please tell us,' says Cow. 'Please tell us everything!'

But Minka is licking one sticky paw. She licks at it and then she pulls at it with her sharp teeth. 'Uuugh! Uuugh!' she cries. 'This is not right!'

She leaps up onto her four feet. 'I must be clean!' says she. 'I cannot tell a story with all this nastiness upon my fur!'

In one dark movement she slides under the edge of the tent and vanishes.

'Ahum,' says Woolly, looking this way and that. 'Dear Ratty, if I may mention it, you are a tadge pongy yourself. This tent is small. We are bound to notice, you know.'

Even Cow, the most polite of cows, wrinkles her nose a bit and blinks her eyes.

'I understand,' says I. 'If I smell like the places I have been to, I must smell nasty indeed.'

I do not wait. I follow Minka out under the tent flap.

Outside the night has come. The wind blows fresh between the tents and huts. There is no sign of Minka.

Cleaning a ratty is not so easy, I must tell you. Minka will look for water. She will be looking at this moment. Then she can swim the dirt away.

But me – swimming is not my thing. You know that. I cannot swim the dirt away. I must rub it and wipe it and scrub it away.

So off I trot to find a damp place that is not wet.

I slide under the fence. Greeber's Ground stretches away into the dark all round me. On one side I see a clump of high shadow that must be trees. Off I bound until I reach the rustling dark under the trees.

I leap forward between their smooth trunks. Here is what I want, leaves, soft leaves.

The ground is thick with leaves that fell last year and the year before. Half-rotted. Deep. Soft. Damp. Smelling clean of earth and air.

There are plants too, spindly and tall, shaking in the night wind. As I bound forward the plants sprinkle dew upon my back.

I start cleaning up in earnest. I dive into the soft leafy earth as if I was Minka diving into cold clean water. I roll upon my sticky back. I rub my head against tree roots. I dig my paws into the clean mud.

I roll and leap and burrow and scratch and rub and shake until my fur is soft and smooth and gleaming.

Last of all I wipe my long and scaly tail through the

thickest wettest grasses that grow at the edge of the tree clump.

Clean at last. No trace of tunnel smell or badness smell. I am the ratty I like to be.

I stand a moment at the edge of the woods. It is dark but not too dark for me to see Minka. She is bounding towards the show fence, a darker shadow in the dark night.

'Minka!' I cry. 'Did you find water?'

She turns and stops and waits for me. I see her white teeth flash as I trot up. The smell of fish hangs round her.

'Oh Ratty,' cries she, 'there is a lake on the far side of the Ground. With ducks and fish too! I have eaten up two fish and am as clean as rain.' She skips a little in the dark.

'And Ratty,' she goes on, 'I am so ashamed. I was so cross in that drain. It was not right. I was not myself you know after my prison box. But to shout at you who had just rescued me! Forgive me!'

'Do not think of it, dear friend,' I say. 'I had forgotten it already. That was a horrid place. But now we are out of it! We are two clean creatures now,' says I. 'Let us forget crossness and find our friends again and tell them what we know.'

So side by side we run forward through the dark and slide into the bright lit tent. Our friends are waiting. Woolly sniffs carefully. A cheerful smile comes over his white and woolly face. 'That is better,' says he. 'Now we can hear your tale.'

'Oh yes,' says Cow. 'Please tell us all that has happened. Who are the Bad Things? How did you find Minka, Ratty? And how did you escape?'

'It is a long story,' says I. 'But we have the night before us. Let us get comfortable.'

So Cow lies down in the thick straw. She takes her time like Cow does. But at last she is settled. Then Woolly flops down. Minka curls up like a shadow in the corner of the tent.

I skip over to where Cow is lying.

I lean back warm against her neck.

And then I tell our story.

CHAPTER 8

It is a long story I have to tell. As I talk on, Cow breathes soft above my head. Woolly stares at me with his bold blue stare. His eyes sparkle when I tell of Chee and the shop and the van. He frowns and flicks his ears when I come to the Bad Things and 29. He snorts through his white nose when I tell of our escape from the glass prison.

At last I have come to the end. 'So here we are,' I say. 'Safe and here with you. But tomorrow is another day. No one can be safe then.'

Cow sighs a deep sigh. I feel the air rush out through her long throat.

'How sad,' says Cow. 'What a sad and cruel story. And 29! I see how he may feel. But it is a cruel thing to take revenge on pets. They have not hurt him.'

'He is half-mad,' says I. 'He thinks he can hurt people that way. He has not thought how cruel it is for other furry things like him. He has not thought.'

'Well I don't care what he thinks!' says Woolly. 'He is being bad and I will fight him and that will be that!' Woolly looks very happy at this. He waves his curly head and flashes his blue eyes.

'I would like to meet Chee,' says Cow.

'You will meet her!' says I. 'She will be here tomorrow for the Show.'

I look over at Minka curled in the corner. She is deep asleep already.

'We should all sleep,' says I. 'Tomorrow is the biggest day ever. We must be ready!'

So this is what we do. Cow settles her big head down upon the straw. I curl up next to her and close my eyes. Woolly closes his bright eyes and snorts. It is sleep time.

Sleep time. Until the first morning light begins to gleam under the tent walls.

When morning comes so does Hat Man. He strides into the tent with food pails in his hand.

'Now here is no surprise!' says he. 'Ratty is back! You knew he would be here I am sure, Cow. I am glad to see you, Ratty.'

At the sound of his voice, Minka wakes. She hisses and leaps backwards.

'Aha,' says Hat Man. 'A wild friend too I see. Do not fear me,' says he to Minka. 'I am a safe sort of person. Your friends will tell you. Anyway I am going now. No need to fret.'

So off he goes again leaving full pails of breakfast for all to eat. Cow gets up onto her four feet. And Woolly too.

Minka is crouching by the tent edge. She is anxious still, I see.

'Hat Man is our friend,' says I. 'Truly you need not fear him. He will help us if he can.'

Minka strokes her whiskers for a moment. Then she steps forward and goes to sit by Woolly.

Cow takes a bite out of one of the pails. She munches and she thinks, all at the same time. 'Adventures are not easy,' says she. 'We know that! This is the day the Bad Things come. We need a plan.'

'The Bad Things will have a plan too,' says I. 'You can be sure of that. There is a lot of them you know. They will have a plan so that they can hurt the pets. Then they will have a plan to get away again.'

Minka rocks slowly and pulls her whiskers. She is thinking hard. '29 will wait,' she says. 'I am sure of that. He will want all the Bad Things to strike together. He is clever.'

'He will want a time when the animals are not guarded,' says I. 'I do not know when that might be. I wish Chee was here. She has been to the Show before. She would know.'

'I do! I do!' cries a voice behind me. 'Of course I do. Hello, new friends. This is me!'

Chee stands just behind me. She has a bright new

collar on with gleamy stones in it. She is brushed smooth and shiny like silk. She is a fine sight to see.

'Pretty eh?' says Chee to me as I stare. 'I shall win the Dog Show I am sure.' Then she turns to the others. 'I am Chee. I am Ratty's friend. I would like to be friends with all of you too. I will be useful, you know.'

Cow is already smiling at her. 'Oh Chee!' says she. 'How pleased I am to meet you. I do not like doggos in general,' says she, 'but Ratty says you are the bravest and the best. Please come and help us and be our friend.'

Woolly steps forward and nods his curly head at her. 'You may be tiny and not so furry neither,' says he, 'but you are a doggo after my own heart. I am proud to meet you.'

'And I am so pleased to meet you,' says Chee. 'Brave Cow and valiant Woolly, heroes both I'm sure. And Minka too! When I met Ratty he was looking for you, Minka.'

So in no time at all we are all sitting together on the straw, talking and planning and being friendly.

'Chee,' I say. 'I want to ask you something. I do not understand, you know. Why are these pets here? I know it is a Show but what is a Show? Why do the people bring their pet friends here?'

'The people come to find who is the best pet,' says Chee. 'They put their pets in cages, or on tables or in pens if they are big. Then another person, who is called a judge, looks at each one. The judge says which is the best pet.'

I stare at Chee. 'How can a pet be a best pet?' says I.

'Well,' says Chee. 'Sometimes the best one is the prettiest one. Sometimes it is the heaviest or the tallest or the cleverest.'

I go on staring. Chee seems to understand it but I do not.

'Woolly and I are getting prizes,' says Cow. 'They are special prizes just for being us.' She goes quite pink and looks at her two front feet.

'I understand that kind of prize,' says I. 'Everyone should have a prize like that! And you are famous after all.'

'You will be more famous by this evening,' sings out Chee. 'And me too! All of us!'

'Not me,' says I. 'Ratties are not famous. It would not be good for me to be famous. But now there is work to do. What is our plan?'

'Well,' says Chee. 'If 29 is clever, like me, he will wait until the end of the day. That is the time when people chat and walk about. Pets are waiting. No one is watching. That will be his best time I am sure!'

'That is hours away,' says Minka. 'The Bad Things have a whole day to creep into the field. A whole day.'

'We must warn the pets,' says I. 'If they are warned they will be safer.'

'I shall be in the Dog Show, you know. I will get a big rosette,' says Chee. 'And while I am there I can warn the doggos and the pups.'

'We need helpers too,' says I. 'We need to find strong creatures who can be our friends. How can we do that?'

'I can do that,' says Cow. 'I can talk to other big things like me. I can ask the other cows and the goats and the sheep to help us.'

Woolly is shaking his curly head and frowning. 'I am not good at talking,' says he. 'There must be something else that I can do.'

'Yes indeed,' says Chee. 'Someone must watch out for the Bad Things. We must know when they creep in. We must know how many there are to fight us. Someone must watch all day through and tell us.'

'That is right,' says I. 'They will come in along the ditch like we did, Minka. That will be the way.

So someone needs to watch that corner of the Show Ground. There are huts down there, and trailers and boxes so it may be hard to see the Bad Things. But someone needs to watch and count if they can.'

'That is me!' cries Woolly. 'I will tell Hat Man to put me in the middle of the Show so I can see that corner. Then I will watch. I can count you know. We sheep are good at counting.'

'I must find my person now,' says Chee. 'She will want me for the Dog Show. You will see me when the fun starts!'

'Fun!' I say to myself. It will be cruel fun, that is what I think.

Chee turns and trots out through the tent door. Cow steps to follow her. 'I will see you later in the day, dear Ratty,' says she. 'Make sure you stay safe, you know.'

'And I will find Hat Man and stand in the middle of the field. Wherever you are, I shall be watching out for you and all the Bad Things too,' says Woolly. His eyes are steely and he snorts through his round white nose. Off he trots after Cow, flicking his curly tail behind him.

'What can I do?' asks Minka.

'The best thing you can do is rest,' says I. 'You are too big to run around the field. You would be caught. But when the fight starts we will need you.'

'There will be a fight?' asks Minka.

'There will be a fight,' says I. 'And a hard fight too. There is no way round it.'

For a moment Minka bares her sharp white teeth and snarls a quiet snarl. Then she closes her shining mouth and nods. 'You are right,' says she. 'I will hide here until I am needed. What will you do, Ratty?'

'I will warn the little animals,' I say. 'The rabbits and the birds and the cats. All the little creatures. They must be warned. I will go now. Safe resting, Minka.'

With that I dodge over to the tent side and stick my brown nose out from under the canvas.

The Show Ground is filling up. I can see people feet and legs. I can smell the animals beyond.

Right in front of me I see a water pipe. It is laid upon the ground and goes straight ahead into the nearest tent. The pipe is covered with rubber matting. There is a nice ratty space under that mat for me.

'I see a way!' I say to Minka over my shoulder. 'All the animals need water. This water pipe will go right round the Ground I am sure. They've put a nice cover on it too – just right for a ratty. Perfect!' says I.

I pause, I listen. And then I go.

Three long bounds and I am squashed in the dark along the pipe. People feet thump nearby. But I am safe.

I squeeze forward. The wet mud sticks to my soft belly fur. A little way further. Then a light appears.

I creep forward. I peer out carefully. Above my head the pipe rises to a tap. I am inside a tent.

It is just as Chee has said. There is a row of cages on long tables. In each cage is a bright and singing bird. The people walk about and look in the cages. They coo. They point. They smile.

The tables are covered over with long cloths that reach the ground. A good place to hide! I dodge under the nearest table.

There is a bird right over my head. I stretch up on my back legs. I whisper up through the table top to the cage above.

'Bird, bird!' I cry.

'Wassat? Wassat?' says a high and chirpy voice. 'Whoosere? Whoosere?'

'A friend,' says I. 'Come to warn you. Bad Things will strike when the day ends. Bad Things to eat you up. Tell your people to lock your cages tight. Stay back from the bars. The Bad Things will come as the people go.'

'Eeeek! eeeek!' trills the little bird high and sharp. 'I will tell them all. Them All! Them All!' He lifts his piercing voice above the hum and chatter of the crowd. He carols out his message across the high tent. 'Bad Things! Bad Things! Lock up! Lock up! Hide! Hide! As People Go!'

All the birds, in every cage, take up the call. They sing out, high or low, sweet or harsh, as their voices are.

'Bad Things! Bad Things! Lock up! Hide!'

The people stop and stare.

'The birds!' they say. 'How loud! How strange! How beautiful!'

The birds call out a warning for all to hear. It carries far over the wide Show Ground.

It carries far – but who will listen? I cannot trust the birds to tell the creatures and keep them safe. It is my job to do and I must find a way to do it.

I scurry under the covered tables to the far side of the tent. I stick my head out into the cool air.

The sun is rising in the sky. The morning is half over and I have just begun.

I look for Woolly.

He is not far away. He sees me. He stares a moment. Then he makes a shape with his tight little mouth.

'Ten,' he mouths at me. 'Ten.'

Ten! Ten Bad Things are here already!

My heart jumps. My paws tremble. Ten Bad Things and so few of us. It is worse than I feared.

Ahead of me is a second tent – and no one watches. I scurry over to it. I dodge in under the canvas flap of the tent. There I lie as still as stone.

Here are more cages. And more long covered tables. Rabbits.

They are already warned, I can see that. Their long

94

ears stand upright on their heads. Their eyes are wide pools of terror.

'Hear the birds!' they whisper to one another. 'Hear the birds!'

'Yes, yes!' I hiss from my corner. 'Make sure your people lock you in tight as tight. Do not jump out! Do not run away! Keep close! Keep safe!'

Their eyes pop in their heads. They shake and tremble.

People are calling out all down the tent. 'What is the matter with the rabbits? And the guinea pigs too? What has frightened them? Poor dears.'

I pull back under the tent edge. I peer out into the crowded green walks between the tents.

The sun shines down stronger than before. It shines clear and bright. But all the time I know the shadow shapes are coming. They creep, and slide, and crawl in every dark place. I am sure of that although I do not see them.

I dodge in behind a lorry wheel. I stare across at Woolly. His eye is on me as it always is. He lifts his white muzzle.

'Twenty,' he mouths at me. 'Twenty.'

Terror comes over me. Twenty Bad Things! So many. So Bad.

And only the birds and rabbits warned. There is much more to do.

It is not easy. I am a strong ratty and a clever ratty, but it is not easy. I go back to my pipe cover. The air under it is hot now. But there is no choice. I squeeze and push along in the hot dark. My eyes sting with the sweat that runs off my furry forehead.

A long push until at last my nose pops out into the bright light of another tent.

Cats!

Now this is harder. Cats and ratties are not such friends, you know. Many a ratty has squeaked his last under a clawed cat paw. But I have my job to do.

The cats are dozing I see. There are no people here neither.

I climb up the table leg and stick my long nose over the edge. Right in front of me is a big white cat. She is fluffy like a dandelion head in autumn. Her eyes are blue and cold and fixed on me. She is in a cage. That is a good thing. If she were out and free, my friends might miss me soon enough.

'SSsssssSSSS,' goes she through her sharp teeth when she sees me. 'What a nasty sight. Someone will

see you, Ratty, and then you will be done in and a good thing too,' says she.

'I have come to warn you,' says I. 'You may not like ratties. No indeed. But I have come to help save you and your kittens there.'

I have seen that on the far side there are kittens. All together in big cages. Mewing and playing and doing what kittens do.

White Cat goes so still that her white waving hair seems to stand stiff and hard like wires off her round back. 'The kittens,' says she. 'What of them? Who threatens them?'

So I tell her. She listens with her white pricked ears and does not move a paw or whisker.

'Who are the Bad Things?' asks she at last.

'All kinds,' says I. 'My kind, and doggos, and ferrets, and your kind too. Kitties with fierce faces and cruel hearts.'

She closes her bright eyes for half a breath. Then opens them again.

'I will believe you,' says she. 'Perhaps there is a good ratty here and there. I shall warn the cats. All the cats will know! Now run,' says she. 'The people will be back soon.'

She pushes slowly to her feet like a white cloud rising. 'Trust me,' says she and I do.

Back I go. I slide down the table leg and back to the tent edge.

Again I point my long nose out and look.

The sun is overhead now. It blazes down upon us all. Time, time is going past. The day is moving over us and the Bad Things gather minute by minute. How can we stop them?

Woolly looks at me from his distant pen. His face is blank and sad. 'Thirty,' he says with his tight white mouth. 'Thirty.'

Thirty Bad Things.

I have told the birds and the rabbits and the cats. Chee has told the doggos I am sure.

Now we must find help. The best, the strongest help. I must find Cow.

I make my ratty way across that crowded Ground. It is not easy at first. But then I reach the pens. Straw is piled thick on the ground. There are blankets and pails and troughs of hay. Just what a ratty needs for hiding. I make my way through all those pens until I find Cow.

She reaches her long muzzle down towards the straw. She sees my eyes gleam but she does not jump or make a sound.

'Dear Ratty,' says she. 'I have done my part. Now we have strong friends to help us fight.'

Five goat heads poke over the next fence. Their curved horns gleam in the sunshine. 'Just show us what to hit,' they say in one long bleat. 'We will do it! We will! We are strong you know and fierce.'

'Thank you,' I say. 'It will be a hard fight but we can win!'

They nod their tasselled heads and blink their strange slit eyes.

Then Cow turns her head the other way. She points her nose over a strong fence that is next to her. 'Our friend here will help us,' says she.

I look up. Then I look higher. I see a long golden wall. A high slab of brown and gold. I look again. It is a fur wall. A living breathing wall. Huge and high and heavy. Strong as Farmer's tractor.

It turns its great head to see me.

Bull! His red-gold head carries short strong horns. A gold ring nods in his nose. His eyes are fringed with pale fur. Gentle eyes. But he is Bull. Bull is gentle just so far and then the fiercest thing in this wide world.

I jump up. I bow politely. 'Dear Bull,' I say. 'How good to meet you. My little ratty eyes did not see you at first. You are the biggest creature I have seen in my short life.'

Bull looks pleased at this. It is true.

'If you are on our side,' says I, 'then perhaps there is hope.'

'I will help you keep the small ones safe,' says Bull. His voice is low and thick and strong. 'Trust me for that.'

'I do,' I say. 'They will need you. At the day's end, it will be. Then we will see what we will see.'

I turn back to Cow. I feel lighter in my heart than I have felt for many a long hour.

'I will find a place to watch,' says I. 'Then we must wait. There is nothing else to do.'

'You could go up there,' says she.

I look up.

There is a high pole by the tents. On the top is a curved box. Out of it a loud voice comes. It is the loud-voice speaker. It looks a nice perch for a ratty. It has the best view of all.

'I will climb up,' says I, 'and watch. I will come down before the fight begins.'

Off I run and scramble and climb to my high perch. I settle down upon it while the soft wind blows around me.

The sun is moving down the sky. It moves so slow but swift enough. Too soon the Show will end. Too soon the people will move and pack their things and go back to their cars.

The time is coming.

I see them now. From my high perch I see the Bad Things.

Behind the rabbit tent a shadow oozes along

the ground. It slips under the edge of the tent. It disappears inside.

Over by the cat tent I see two heads lift for a moment, then drop again. A kitten voice calls out, 'Who is there? Is it my mother come for me?'

By the tent where the bright birds are, three sleek shapes slide along the ground. They disappear into the shadows beyond.

These are the ones I see and there are many more. The time has come.

The pets call out to each other. 'Remember!' calls a guinea pig. 'Remember the Bad Things!'

'Away from the bars! Away! Away!' sings a bird.

But the people don't know. I see one person lift down a pair of brindled puppies. She sets them on their feet. Off they stagger over the wet ground on their red leads. The puppies have forgotten. They are only puppies.

A single rabbit hops out of his cage onto the table

top. Perhaps he did not hear the warning.

'Get back! Get back!' hiss his friends. He looks around him puzzled. He does not understand.

All the tents are being cleared now. There are cages on the ground. Pet owners walk here and there. They meet old friends. They stop and chat. They leave their pets with no one to guard them.

And so the Bad Things come.

CHAPTER 9

The Bad Things are here.

A scream floats up from far over the field. 'Aah! Something has bitten my dog! Get away! Get away!'

It has begun.

I slide down the high pole. As my four feet hit the ground, I hear a yell from the bird tent. 'Mad cats are here! And ferrets! Down! Away with you! Help! Help! They'll eat the birds!'

There is a great crash in the bird tent. A splintering of wood. A cracking of wire. Out of the wide tent door flies a cloud of birds, a coloured stream of tiny birds. Up into the darkening sky. I see a cat slide out from under the tent edge. There is a feather in its mouth.

From the rabbit tent a sobbing voice cries out, 'Oh Suky Rabbit! Suky Rabbit! Dear Suky, someone has bitten you.' A person runs out of the tent. In her arms is a big rabbit. One ear hangs over its face. There are red bite marks on its neck. It blinks a shocked eye at me.

'The Bad Things,' it whispers.

Now I see them everywhere.

Dark shadows leap and bound across the grassy spaces between the tents. They pour in from the field edge.

The pale shape of a grey dog hunts past me. His nose is to the ground. 'I smell kittens!' he snarls. 'And rabbits too!'

'No!' I squeal in my high ratty voice. 'No! You will not hurt the kittens! You will not hurt the rabbits! Stop him! Stop them all!'

My voice calls out amongst the screaming and the wild hubbub. But another voice is stronger.

From the pens I hear it. A roar like the sea. 'Now! Now!' bellows Bull.

The roar rumbles far out over the Ground. It shakes the tents. It makes the fences tremble.

'Now!' roars that great and mighty voice. Bull is roused. And he brings others with him.

With two blows of his great head he strikes the fence of his pen. It breaks into a thousand pieces. Out of his pen comes Bull.

Smash! He cracks open the next fence and the next. The goats and sheep are free. They come running in Bull's wake.

The sheep whisk their tails. They kick and prance with their forked feet. The goats wave their horned heads to the sky and bleat with fierce voices.

Here is Chee high on a goat's back. She waves her yellow tail. 'Fight! Fight!' she shouts.

Cow is here too. There is a hard glow in her gentle eyes. 'Save the pets! Save them!' she cries. 'Save them from the Bad Things.'

Here comes Woolly Woolly Baa Lamb. His cold blue eyes are wild and happy. He dances on his hard little hooves. 'Where are the Bad Things? Let me fight them! Let me hit them with my hard head!' he bleats.

Then he sees them. On every side they run. Swift shadows. Cruel shapes. They run, they leap, they bite, they bay for blood.

I see four rats like me – oh shame! They have seized a fluffy dog. They are trying to pull him down onto the ground. They bite him with their sharp teeth and hang from his long fur.

'Aaaah!' screams the owner.

'Yiiiip! Yiiiip! I am hurt!' squeals the dog.

Crash! Here comes Woolly Woolly Baa Lamb. He thunders past me. He pauses. He stares with his cold blue eyes. He turns a little. Then his two back legs lash out like two steel hammers. Each hard back foot hits a rat.

Wheeeee! Up they go. High into the air. Thud. They land upon the ground. Their eyes roll in their rat heads. 'Where am I?' whispers one of them.

There are two rats left. They do not wait. They leave go of the dog's fluffy sides. They drop to the ground. They run for safety. Woolly is after them.

'Aaaah!' cry the rats. They are the ones who scream now.

'You brave sheep!' cries the dog person. 'Brave sheep. Kind sheep!'

Woolly gallops off after the rats. 'I will get you I will, I will, I will,' snorts he.

I run on. Into the bird tent. The bird cages are tumbled down. The cage doors have sprung wide. The birds have flown. Except one.

A cat has got here first. A striped cat. A big cat. It reaches forward into the bird's cage with its clawed paw.

'No! No!' I squeak.

'Yes! Yes!' snarls the cat.

I rush forward. But past me, over me, comes a rushing leaping shape.

It is Minka.

'No!' screams Minka. She hurtles forward like a cannon ball. Her white teeth flash. She seizes the fluffy end of the cat's tail. With a yell, the cat turns. He pulls back out of the cage. He faces Minka.

'Fight someone your own size. Fight me!' says Minka, through the fluff of the furry tail.

That would be all right if Minka was cat-size but she is not. The cat is a big cat. He is twice as tall as Minka and twice as heavy. He has sharper claws and bigger teeth. I do not like the look of this.

'If that's what you want!' snarls the cat.

His long claws gleam and slash. Red lines appear on Minka's back. She lets go of his tail.

It is not a fair fight. He is twice her size. He is twice her weight.

But Minka is a wild wild thing and he is hearth bred.

'Yip yee!' sings Minka in her throat. It is the killing cry of the wild mink. It freezes my blood. Her eyes glow red. Her mouth snarls open. Every sharp tooth is there to see.

'Yip yee!' she calls again. Then she leaps. Like a black wave. Like night falling. She leaps onto the cat. She sinks her teeth into his throat.

'Oh my!' I squeak. 'No killing. No more blood. Please. Oh help!'

Thud. Thud. It is Cow galloping up to help. She sees at a glance what is happening. The cat is on his back. His eyes bulge. His paws wave weakly in the air.

'Minka!' bellows Cow. So loud that the tables shake. 'Minka. Dear Minka. Let him live!'

Minka lifts her wild face. She looks at us. The red glow dies in her eyes. She loosens her grip. She steps back. She trembles with fury and the lust for blood.

'Thank you,' says she. 'Thank you for stopping me. Oh Cow, I do not want to be as bad as them. But this is a cruel cruel cat.'

He is a sad cat now. That is what I think. He lies a moment on his back. His breath whistles in his throat. Then he rolls onto his side. He struggles to his feet.

He looks at us for a moment. Then he shakes his head and turns away. Slowly, slowly, he walks towards the tent door. 'Home,' he mutters to himself. 'Home.'

In the tumbled cage, the bird pulls his golden head from under his wing. He blinks his black eyes. He chirps a quiet chirp.

One creature saved. But what about the rest?

'The rabbits! The kittens!' I cry. 'The Bad Things are everywhere!'

'This way!' calls Minka.

Off we run. Cow pauses for a moment. She looks down at me.

'Hop up!' says she. I run up her leg and settle on her broad head. 'Old times,' says Cow. She smiles her soft smile.

'Dear Cow,' says I. 'Old times indeed.'

'Let's go!' says Cow. She leaps forward on her strong legs. She crashes out through the tent door into the open air.

Then we see.

The biggest tent is ahead of us. It is not like a tent any more. It is more like a white balloon, bulging, pulling, bouncing, twisting, leaning.

From inside we hear a great noise.

We hear the high squeals of rabbits and guinea pigs. The growls and snarls of dogs. The hiss of ferrets. The sharp squeaks of fighting rats.

And above it all, the roar of Bull.

In through the door we go. Crash! Bull's head smashes a table. It splits into two pieces. It flies in splinters through the air. Crash again! Bull's head strikes another table.

The Bad Things shout out with fright at Bull's hard horns and his bright eye.

Forward he steps again. Down goes his head. He flicks the next table sideways with his horns. Under it cower three dogs and a ferret. Their eyes stare upward wide and blank with fear.

'Go!' snorts Bull. He kneels down upon his mighty knees to get his head down to them. 'Go!'

They do not wait. As his great horns sweep by them they turn and flee.

'Go! Go!' he bellows.

They go. And all their friends go with them.

Bull rises from his knees. He flashes his bright eye this way and that.

'Where are my enemies?' he says. 'Where?'

They have fled.

The sweat pours off Bull's great golden sides. The breath comes in heavy snorts from his round nostrils. Two people are cowering in a corner but they step forward now.

'Oh brave bull!' they say. 'You have saved our pets.' They run to find their pets and hold them tight.

It is brave work. It is. The Bad Things are beaten here. But here is not everywhere.

Where is Number 29? In all this time and strife I have not seen him.

I look this way and that.

Number 29 is here. He must be. His cruel heart has set this all in motion. He is here.

But where?

I slide down from Cow's head and leap onto the ground. 'I will be back,' I whisper. 'I have work to do!'

I scamper out of the tent. I look. I listen.

There is still fighting here and there. Woolly bursts out from the kitten tent. Rat shapes flee before him. He snorts and shakes his head. Then he sees me and winks his blue eye. I run on.

Somewhere. Somewhere. He is here somewhere. Number 29.

I turn a corner. Then I stop.

I am almost at the big gate now. By the gate is a square of paved ground. People have stacked cages against the wall. They have left them there to collect and gone for their cars. Out from the cages peer rabbits. Their eyes are round and full of fright.

In front of the cages is a dark furred shape.

He is standing tall on his hind legs. Peering. Looking. Waiting.

The pale rabbit faces stare out. I hear their sobbing breaths.

They stare at him.

Him. Number 29. Big and fierce and beautiful as ever. He stands tall upon his back legs and he sways. His head weaves to and fro.

There is something strange here. That I can see. Something new, something odd.

His red eyes glow – but not with rage. Not with cruel revenge neither. No. With grief. With sadness.

'What have I done?' he whispers.

He sways again. He clenches his front paws tight together.

'I have hurt the caged things. I have hurt the pets. Caged things like me.'

He sways again. The rabbits stare back in terror.

'I have turned into a cruel person-thing. I am like them!' he howls. The sound flies high and lamenting into the darkening sky.

The rabbits cling to each other. They sob. The tears run down their furred faces.

'I should not be out here,' says he. 'I cannot live so. I cannot live without my cage. I need a cage.'

He drops onto his four feet and steps forward. One of the cages is empty. He leans his head against the wire. His paws clutch the mesh.

The tears flow from his red eyes. They drop onto the stone slabs beneath.

The people are coming now. They are moving forward between the cars. One of them has a net.

The dark mink head presses close against the mesh. The wire makes deep squares in his plush dark fur.

'Let me in. Let me in,' he whispers.

The net drops.

I watch a moment more. Number 29 does not struggle. He lies in his net peering out through the squares. I even think his face is peaceful now.

'Caught. Trapped. Caged,' he whispers. 'At last!'

Then he closes those glowing eyes. He curls into a shining ball of fur. And two men carry him away.

I turn to go. I run wearily over that wide field. As I go I see the last of the Bad Things. They are here and there and everywhere.

But they are uncertain now. They look around them. Where is their leader? Where is 29? They divide and falter. One head turns, then another. Where is he?

Where is he?

Then they see the bundled net. They see that gleam of fur. They see those closed eyes and that still shape.

They turn. They flee.

The battle is over. The Bad Things have fled. I am a weary ratty. I scamper back to find my friends.

At last I find Cow. She is smiling her happy smile and watching the little birds fly down from their cold tree. The bird people call and wave food. One by one the golden shapes come skimming down.

Chee is here. Her person is holding her tight. 'What a naughty doggo this is,' says Chee's person to

Cow. 'Always running away.' She strokes Chee's head and cuddles her tighter still. 'But she always comes back,' says she.

Chee winks her round eye at me and smiles.

The rabbits are all back in their cages. They look pleased to be there. The kittens are playing in a circle on the floor. None of them is hurt. A vet is going here and there. He looks carefully at all the animals, patching the ones who need it.

'Nothing serious,' says he with a smile.

Here is Woolly Woolly Baa Lamb. He is dancing on his hard hooves and bleating loud and long.

'We beat them. We fought them. How brave! How wonderful we are!' says he. And who can say that he is wrong?

I look about me. It is people time now. There are cameras and bright flashes and talking and best of all here comes Hat Man. He has Minka in his arms.

'Well friends,' says he. 'A good day's work! I shall never know the whole of it I suppose but I know enough. Minka here says there is another mink to find. Lost and sad and needing help.'

'Yes indeed,' says I. 'They have him in a net by the gate.'

'Aha!' says Hat Man. 'I'll just give Minka to the vet and then I'll be off.' He strides over and explains to the vet. Then out he goes.

I sink down upon a patch of straw. 'Oh Cow,' says I. 'I am a tired ratty. Sleep is next.'

So there and then I close my eyes. While Cow stands by me to keep me safe.

CHAPTER 10

Back to the Farm we go at last. All piled into Hat Man's trailer.

There are two extra shapes wrapped in sacking which lie upon the floor but who is to know? Who is to say?

'We need not tell anyone that we have mink friends at the farm now,' says Hat Man. 'This is something I will keep under my hat!' Then he chuckles all the way back to the Farm.

Minka does not stay wrapped up for long. As soon as we stop and the door opens, she crawls out and blinks her black eyes.

'I am stiff and sore,' says she, 'but soon I will be right as rain I know.'

She is right. The cat's claws cut deep wounds but they will heal soon enough.

Other scars are deeper. Hat Man carries 29 from the trailer into the back of Cow's shed.

And there he stays. For day after day. For week after week.

Minka is well much sooner. She skips about the Farm when visitors have gone. She dives into the duck-pond after dark until the ducks complain to Hat Man. She chats with Chee who visits every week now with her person. But it is not enough. Minka is bored.

So one bright day she asks Hat Man to take her to the river and we see her no more.

Not 29.

For long weeks he lies in the dark in Cow's shed. Some days the red fire returns and glows in his eyes. On those days he grinds his white teeth and hides his head beneath his paws.

But other days the fire dies away. Those days he lies and sleeps and talks to anyone who visits him. And all the time Cow keeps her gentle eye upon him. Some nights she hums a cow song to him when the bad dreams come. I hear it float faint through the night air. Not many ratties, nor people neither, can boast of hearing that.

But at last, at last, the day comes when 29 crawls out and lies behind the shed. He has had enough of roofs and walls. He stares up at the sky clear above him.

After that he comes out every day.

Hat Man builds a fence so that visitors do not glimpse even the tip of 29's dark furred tail.

'Visitors do not need to know,' says Hat Man.

One bright day I see 29 peering over Hat Man's

fence with cool calm eyes. He rubs his paws along his shining whiskers.

'What now?' says he. 'What next?'

He cannot stay here now that he is well.

So into the trailer once more we go. And here we are.

On the wide river shore where the sea and river meet. Watching.

I am perched high on Cow's head. Woolly Woolly Baa Lamb is a short way off. He is munching green grass. He keeps his bright eye on everything that happens.

On the edge of the river bank is Hat Man and one of his helpers. They are digging out a deep hole in the long bank. 29 is close by. He is standing tall on his back legs and peering at the hole in the bank. He is puzzled.

Next to us lies a heavy wooden hutch. It is like a rabbit hutch but much bigger. One half is caged in with wire mesh. The other half is open at the front.

Hat Man finishes digging the hole. He comes over with his helper. They carry the hutch over to the bank.

Hat Man turns to 29.

'You want to be free I know,' says Hat Man, 'but some days fear comes. On those days you need a cage to hide in. Well,' says Hat Man, 'this box can be your safe place. If you feel frightened, you can come here. As soon as you are strong again, you can run out onto the riverside. You will be free and safe too.'

Number 29 listens. He nods his shining head. His dark fur blows and glistens in the wind. His eyes are bright now. The red fire in them has died.

Hat Man pulls the hutch forward. He and the helper push it into the space in the bank. They pile the dark earth around it and tread it down.

'That will do nicely,' says Hat Man. 'In a week or two it will be part of the bank. You'll see,' says he.

Minka is further down the shore. She is playing through the shallow water. Suddenly she leaps and pounces. I see the flash of silver as she catches the fish. Down her throat it goes. Double quick.

'Shells and fisshes
How delisshus!'

She sings out.

She dances a dance of triumph on the wild river shore.

Hat Man and Helper trudge back to the van for their sandwiches. They have done their work for today.

'Let us have a look,' says I.

So Cow and Woolly and I step forward to look at 29's new home.

'It is fine, is it not?' he says. His voice is softer than it was in that dark tunnel where I met him first. 'I shall be safe here.'

He looks round him at the wide and empty shore. 'Perhaps I shall not need my cage,' says he. 'Perhaps I shall not feel frightened at all.'

'There is lots of space here,' says Cow. 'No people. No pets. A mink place. A wild place.'

'You are right,' says he. 'There is space here for all us wild things. And I have my friend too,' he says. He looks along the shore to where Minka runs and plays. 'All will be well,' says he.

'All will be well,' says Cow smiling.

Woolly is peering at the river running by.

'This river,' says he. 'We swam it once. Cold and wet it was. But I would like to look at it again.'

We trot across to the rippling river edge. Woolly steps into the water. Very carefully. Just until it covers his hard little hooves.

'We did it!' he bleats out. 'We did it! And we are safe now!'

Number 29 smiles a dark and whiskered smile. I think it is the first time I have seen him smile.

'Perhaps we are all safe now,' says he. He hisses in a pleased sort of way and bounds off up the beach to join Minka in the waves.

Cow steps forward. She leans her long neck down so that I am hanging over the running water. She takes another step. The cold river ripples past her knees.

She looks across to the far shore. Then turns her head to where the city lies beyond the bridge.

'Safe now,' she says.

And so we stand on the cold river's edge, while the wild mink play and the wind blows out to the sea. Until Hat Man waves to us and home we go.